T0064439

Listen to
Heart

Listen to Heart

AAKASH PUNATAR

PARTRIDGE
A Penguin Random House Company

To order additional copies of this book, contact
Partridge India
000 800 10062 62
orders.india@partridgepublishing.com

www.partridgepublishing.com/india

Contents

Prologue

Tuesday, October 28, 2008

Diwali Day, when the world was celebrating the Festival of Light. I was sitting inside the ICU for Rohit, one of my best friends. Oops! I can say, my brother. Few hours back, everything was fine, but as is said, life is unpredictable.

Rohit and I were planning for drinks after the meeting at the office, and then we both headed to the Blue Moon Pub at Brigade Road. As soon as we enter the pub, a beautiful voice hits us. It's Priya, who was singing, 'Tinka tinka zara zara hai roshani se jaise bhara.' It was almost our daily routine to go to the Blue Moon Pub, especially for Rohit.

I think God was high when he created Priya, because there's no one else who comes so close to perfection! Whenever Priya sings, she's breathlessly refreshing. Her smile lights the darkness of heart; her voice leaves you with goose bumps all over. She was a perfect example of beauty with a brain. I usually used to write over there, as I love the darkness, and Rohit used to listen to Priya without blinking his eyes.

Priya was a talented girl but works at the Blue Moon Pub to earn her daily bread. Anyone who sees her will obviously fall in love, with her simplicity and of course at her voice. Blue Moon Pub was famous for music with alcohol at Bridge Road. Many different kinds of people visit the pub daily, but

Rohit has a reason to visit daily as he loves Priya lots. For others, she is just a singer or some even say call girl or bad girl, but Rohit loves her from the bottom of his heart. Sometimes we can't see the pain behind the smile. She is just doing this job at the pub to support her family, and if someone sings in the pub, there is nothing wrong, but you can't control others' thought process.

After the pub closed, Rohit was waiting for Priya to come outside. I was just having my smoke near my bike. I saw the lovely couple from afar, but today I felt something was missing in their meeting. Priya looked tense, and from a distance I could see that she was crying. Rohit was trying to console her. After a couple of minutes, Rohit came back and asked me to drop him back home. While going back home, he was not talking; he was looking calm but tensed. I dropped him and came back to home. I had a headeacheas I had taken five bottles of beer there. I immediately felt asleep.

City Hospital: At 3 a.m. I got a call from a city hospital. I was not in my senses, but then I gathered enough courage to listen properly. I was hardly able to listen from the other side that Rohit was in serious condition and his last dialled number was mine, so they called me. It was a shock for me. I rushed to the hospital at light speed. It took twenty-two minutes for me to reach there, but those twenty-two minutes were like twenty-two years.

The coffee vending machine's sound broke my thoughts. I was still waiting for a surgeon to come. When things go wrong, you feel so miserable, and all you wish for is to completely erase the bad memories. When things are not under your control, you feel so helpless before your so-called destiny.

Imperial Institute of Technology 2002

Friday, June 14, 2002

Rohit was continuously looking at his huge desktop screen for our entrance exam result. Today our fate would decide where to head for graduation. Eighth of May we had appeared for an exam. I applied through sports quote, as I knew I couldn't clear the entrance exam without my sports quote.

I was a state football player. On 7 May, before the final written round, I had played under sports quote to get a 100 per cent score of the sports quote to be considered with the written exam score. On the eighth of May, Rohit and I gave the test. He was hoping to top the exam, as he was an intelligent and bright student. I was hoping to clear the exam, as I played well in the sports round. I had scored three goals for my team.

I was yelling at him that he should not to take so much tension, but Rohit kept refreshing the browser. I was having my beer, the most beautiful thing God has ever created on this planet earth. Suddenly Rohit jumped with joy. I got up and looked at the screen.

'Rohit Vaishnav, 4 GPA—secure first rank, Imperial institute of Technology.' He hugged me tightly. I can see tears rolling from his eyes. Finally, I entered my roll number.

'Rahul Jain, 4 GPA Sports Quote, 3 GPA Written Quote, Imperial institute of Technology.'

I couldn't believe this! I checked my name more than ten times to verify. God fulfilled my wish, and both of us got into the same college.

July 3, 2002

We were at Ahmedabad Station 7 in the morning. Rohit was fully excited. His dream to become a master in computer science had just begun. I had mixed feeling, as I was never serious for studies. My target was very clear: to finish the course without any backlog and get into any good MNC.

Around 10 a.m., we reached the campus, and I was surprised to see such a beautiful campus. Especially since it had a football ground. Hostel Warden assigned room F26 for us. As soon as we entered the room, I just jumped to my bed. F26, our adda for the next three years! I can say it was our territory and we were the kings of F26.

F26 was not as bad as I had thought. First-year students were allocated rooms on the ground floor of the hostel building. There was a long corridor with a series of rooms one after the other. F26 had two single beds with an attached washroom. Apart from wooden beds with cotton mattresses and pillows, two separate small steel almirahs were there. A small dressing table in one corner of the room was giving a scary look. Latest movie star posters were hanging on the wall above the bed, probably put up by the previous occupants. The canteen was on the same floor and had fixed meal timings.

Our class started on the next day, 4 July, coincidentally on American Independence Day. What a day to start the college!

July 4, 2002, 9.00 a.m.

Future computer engineers were ready to fight a battle with books in their hands. Rohit was sitting on the first bench as usual and I was in search of hot chicks, but my fate was never good when it came to girls. Almost everyone had come and settled down in the classroom before time. Few minutes later a man in his mid sixties and looking very strict entered and introduced himself as our HOD. All students stood up to greet him. Before he could start the introduction about the great institute, a beautiful voice interrupted him. 'Can I come in, sir?' He ignored the voice after listening, but all boys were looking outside to spot the nice voice. Boys will always be boys. I smiled at this thought. She waited for a couple of seconds and again asked for permission to enter. He gave her a very annoyed look and allowed her, with a warning to the class that he didn't like late comers. Only one place was vacant—that, too, next to Rohit; she sat there. Except Rohit, all were staring at her. She wasn't beautiful like Angelina Jolie but had some spark in her personality which could attract anybody. After she settled down, Mr HOD started his speech.

'I am Professor Ranganath, HOD of the department. Next three years, me and my staff will make you better! No, best computer engineers. By the time you are in fifth semester, around 120 software companies would come to hire you. So show the best in you. All the best.' As soon as he left the class, Rohit glanced at her for the first time, and something sparked. Students were waiting for the first lecture after the boring speech by Professor Ranganath. Everyone was introducing one another, but Rohit doesn't know how and where to start an introduction with the girl sitting next to him. I stood up from the last bench and came to Rohit and asked him to come with me to the canteen. He was kind of lost and speechless, as if he was not in his senses. He was behaving like he was seeing God's beautiful creation called girl for the first time. Yes, both of us have studied in a boy's school, so we have never had any experience with girls. But I never expected that Rohit would behave like this. I asked him again, this time with a high voice, 'Do you want to come for tea?' After listening to my voice, he finally came to senses, back to the real world, and stood up. We left the class and went to the canteen for tea. Rohit didn't want to bunk lecture on the first day, so we went back to class again. Still all students were waiting for the first lecture. Rohit was back to his seat next to the raving beauty, and I returned to my last bench.

Finally at 10 a.m., a lady assistant professor entered the class. She was in her early thirties and looking beautiful. She gave a brief introduction about her. Her name was Kiran, and she would take care of our data structure topics. I didn't know what data structure was; I just knew structure with curves. She was so beautiful that if I were not a student, I would have proposed to her then and there.

After four lectures back to back, all the students looked tired. At 2 p.m., Rohit and I went to the canteen for our lunch. Rohit still looked lost. I only heard of and seen love at first sight in movies, but after having a crush on Miss Kiran,

I could understand Rohit's condition. At 3 p.m., we reached our room, F26. Before we could open the door, a bunch of seniors were waiting for us. I understood the situation; they were here for ragging. They had called all first-year students to gather in one of the seniors' room named Raja Bhaiya. He was looking like Kadar Khan in his early movies. He ordered all of us to introduce ourselves in pure Hindi. Depending on the number of mistakes in the introduction, they would give different tasks to us, and we had to do that accordingly. It was my turn. I started the introduction.

'Mera Naam Rahul Jain, Pitaji ka Naam Gyanendra Jain.' Till this point, everything was going smoothly, but how do I say that I had done bachelor's in computer science in Hindi? I said it in English. After my introduction, the result was announced. Thirty-six mistakes! And the punishment was to visit the girls' hostel in the night and go to room no. G78, Miss Anita's room, who was Raja Bhiya's girlfriend, and collect a book from her and give it to Raja Bhiya. As you know, boys are not allowed in the girls' hostel. So it was a very difficult task, but somehow I was giggling to myself by thinking about the girls' hostel. Rohit looked little jealous of me, as he wanted to go to the girls' hostel and know about that gorgeous girl. After returning from a ragging session, I googled what BCA was called in Hindi. We brought Rohit's desktop from home. I was shocked to see the result; it was कंप्यूटर अनुप्रयोग स्नातक (बीसीए) .

First Trouble

After spending one beautiful month, it was time for our first internal. According to me, it is a very wrong method to evaluate what students learn in a short period of time. I feel in India, exams only screw the system. Students just give the exam to score marks, not to showcase their knowledge. In India, education is directly linked to the job. If we do not study hard, we won't get a good job. But I can't change this system, so I have to fall with our educational system.

Rohit was finally able to get a name of the mysterious girl. Her name was Rashmi, and she was from Madhya Pradesh, staying in a hostel with Shruti. Shruti was our classmate. From childhood, Rohit was very bright student. For him, exam was not a big deal. He never mug up things like me or any other student, but he understands the process, so for him it is very easy to score. After the class, Rohit used to spend most of his time at the library. I used to joinehim in between. At night, he used to give his revision lecture to me, and then I used to pick the important topic. We both were ready for the exam. We had daily two papers, one in the morning and one in the afternoon. Internal was scheduled for three days. In the first semester, we had in total five subjects and one practical lab.

Finally, internal was over. We decided to have a party. Gujarat is a dry state, but Raja Bhiya had enough contacts to arrange for the alcohol. Rohit and I locked the room from inside for our first alcohol party inside our kingdom of F26. 'Rohit, please play some good songs,' I requested of him while having my beer.

After having two bottles each, suddenly Rohit said, 'I love you, Rashmi.' It was the very first time I was seeing Rohit like this. Love is the seventh sense of humans which can destroy all other six senses. When you are in love, everything looks so colourful. Rohit started his desktop and opened his Orkut page. He was searching for Rashmi on Orkut but could not get her account. Poor boy.

Next morning, Mr Ranganath, HOD, entered into the class with the results. 'Good morning, students, I am here to announce the result. I want to declare our first three rank holder. Rohit Vaishnav, congratulations, you stood first.' He declared the other two names, which are not important to me. Another student can check their report on the notice board. Professor Ranganath left the room. I came from my last bench and hugged my best buddy for his success. All were congratulating Rohit for his success. Suddenly out of all students, Rohit heard a beautiful voice.

'Congratulation, Rohit. You deserve this.' It was her, Rashmi. Rohit delivered a smile to her; she forwarded her hand to wish him.

The first touch of Rashmi sent shivers down Rohit's spine. I was seeing this beautiful scene from a distance. For Rohit, everything looked like a still frame. He was in his imagination, where only he and Rashmi existed on this planet. The five-second handshake made Rohit speechless. After this wonderful scene, I came out to check my result on notice board. I had secured 68 per cent. For me, 68 per cent was the top of the world. All thanks went to Rohit, who always helped me in the studying, which I hated the most.

Seniors arranged a small party at Raja Bhiya's room to celebrate Rohit's success.

Time flew very fast; we were ready for our second internal. This time Rohit was preparing really well. We both reached the library, and at our regular table Rashmi and Shruti were sitting. Rashmi looked so graceful in her dress. She was wearing a knee-length, blue one-piece dress and had left her hair loose, with a few strands falling on her face. She was hardly wearing any make-up except a slight lip gloss and very light blue eyeliner. You should see the spark in Rohit's eyes. Boy was in love. I could feel the love in the air. After we settled down, Rashmi asked Rohit to solve the complex data structure problem. He solved it very easily. I decided to leave the library and allow my friend to spend some time with Rashmi. But how can I convey the same message to Shruti!

The second internal results were out, Rohit topped the exam again. Slowly he was becoming the professors' favourite. This time I secured 73 per cent. I patted my back. I decided not to give the third internal and focus on the final exam. While on another side Rohit was preparing fully for the third internal and final exams. Third internal was around the corner. I wanted to give just two papers to improve my score. In the other three subjects, I secured more than 70 per cent scores. Rohit secured more than 90 per cent in all the subjects, but still he was planning to write all papers. As usual, Rohit topped the third internal also. Everybody, including HOD, had faith that Rohit would secure first rank in the university for his final first-semester exam.

Reading Time

Fifteen days were given to us for reading preparations for the final exam. Everything was going great, but life is never certain, and it is very fragile.

The hostel warden came in search of Rohit. I opened the door in my half sleep. Warden told me it was a call for Rohit from his house. Rohit had left the room in the early morning and went to the library for study. As the phone was on hold, I had decided to go to the hostel office and pick up the phone. It was Aunty. I greeted her. She was crying. It gave me a shock to hear Aunty's low voice. She told me Rohit's father got a heart attack and asked me to inform Rohit. I hung up the phone and ran to the library. Rohit was looking very calm and reading for a final exam. I held myself back, looking at Rohit. We all should have undo capacity. I wished to rewind life by one day. It was so perfect till yesterday night. Finally, I gathered courage and called him out. I didn't know how to say this news to him. He came out along with me. I informed him that 'Uncle got a heart attack and you have to go to your home'. He looked so shocked after this horrible news. He immediately started crying. I somehow managed him and asked him to come to our room first. On the way to the hostel, we met up with Rashmi. She greeted Rohit. Rohit couldn't reply as he was in shock. She just looked at Rohit's wet eyes. I didn't have time to explain anything to anybody. I also ignored Rashmi that time. I just held Rohit and entered our room. I helped him pack his luggage. I switched on Rohit's desktop and opened the browser to check the available flight for Jaipur. The earliest flight was in the afternoon. I booked a ticket for him.

We just left the room and came to the hostel gate. I wanted to drop him at the airport to give him moral support. I took an auto from our hostel gate. On the way, Rohit didn't utter a word. He was still crying. I just hugged him. Sometimes a simple hug can reduce tons of burdens. 'Don't worry. Uncle will be fine. Don't take much tension. If you behave so low, think about Aunty. Be strong, everything will be all right.' I dropped him off at the airport and returned to the room. Life is so unpredictable. Rohit topped all the internals exam, and before final exam Uncle got an attack. How could this happen to Rohit? I was feeling tense and didn't want to sit alone in the room, so I decided to go to the library. Anyhow, now this time I had to read a little hard, as Rohit was not there to help me. I was not worried about my exam. I only worried about Uncle's health and Rohit's exam. As soon as I entered the library and settled at our regular reading table, Rashmi came to me. She looked worried about Rohit. She asked me why Rohit was crying. 'Rohit's dad got a heart attack,' I informed her.

Before I finished the line, she asked another question. 'When will he return for the exam?' She was more worried about Rohit's exam rather than Uncle. But I couldn't judge her. Even I didn't have the right to judge her.

'I don't know how serious Uncle is,' I told her. Even in the library I couldn't be able to focus on the study. At night, I called Rohit and asked him about Uncle's health. He was sounding so low. He again started crying over the phone. I wanted to be with him now. Sometimes we feel so helpless. I could understand Rohit's pain.

'Uncle still in ICU,' Rohit informed me. Rohit is an only child. He had to be there at this time, but I was worried about his exam also, as he was a bright student and everybody in the department had high hopes for him. I didn't want Rohit's full year to be dropped because of this. I was praying to God for Uncle's health. 'Don't cry, Rohit, please be strong. You are the one who has to give strength to all, so please be strong and face the situation. I am with you.'

Five days to go for the exam. I called Rohit. Aunty picked up the phone. I greeted her and asked about Uncle's health. Aunty informed me that by evening Uncle would be discharged and Rohit was in the hospital for finishing all the formalities and would return for the exam by tomorrow. I felt so relieved.

I reached the airport to pick up Rohit. He was looking so tired. I hugged him tightly. 'Now don't worry. Uncle is at home and he is fine now. You please focus on the exam as just three days to go.' After the bath, Rohit picked up all his books and headed towards the library with me. Rohit looked tense but calm. After an hour, I left the library for my smoke. Rohit was studying hard to cover up the week's loss. As soon as I reached the main gate, Rashmi greeted me and enquired about Rohit. I informed her that he had just returned this morning and was in the library. I don't know why, but I didn't want Rohit to focus elsewhere then. I returned to the library a few minutes later. Rohit was missing, but he left his books at the table only, and I was not able to see Rashmi also. I wondered where Rohit was! I had come out in search of him, but he was nowhere. I returned to the library; still Rohit had not come. I wanted Rohit to study as hard as possible. I wanted to see him at the first position in exam results. I had decided to search for him. I again left the library after keeping my books and came to the canteen. He was not in the canteen also. Then I came to our practical lab but couldn't be able to trace him. Finally, I decided to wait at the library only. While on the way to the library, I saw him with Rashmi at the college garden. I didn't want to disturb him, but I didn't want him to waste time now. I don't know why I was feeling like that. I was the one who wanted Rohit to express his feelings for Rashmi. But today, when I was seeing both of them together for the first time, I wanted him to focus on his study. I was seeing both of them from the distance. Suddenly Rohit started crying like a small boy. I was about to go there, but then somehow I controlled myself and decided to leave from that place. I came to the library and started reading. After a few minutes, later Rohit and Rashmi joined me. Rohit looked a little relaxed than before. Rashmi also joined us for study. Sometimes it is not bad to cry over the situation; obviously, it won't serve any purpose, but it would surely reduce the tons of burden which is on the heart.

Exam Day!

Rohit looked more confident than he was three days before. In the last two days, Rashmi gave him confidence, which he required the most. Rohit and I prayed to God and left the hostel at 8.30 a.m. to reach our exam hall. I was not nervous, but there was some anxiety. We reached the exam hall at 8.40a.m. Rashmi and Shruti both were standing there. Rashmi forwarded her hand and wished Rohit good luck. After five days, exams were over.

It was time to go home after six months. We had already booked the ticket to the train, but it was for the next day. I was full in the party mood. I asked Rohit to do the party all night. I wanted him to smile and forget every tension which he had passed in the last fifteen days. Rohit became a very silent kind of person after Uncle's heart attack. He didn't have any mood for the party, but he wouldn't want to disappoint me, so he agreed to the party.

Semester Off

27 November 2002

I was very excited to go home after six months. We had booked the ticket for the Ahmedabad–Jaipur express train. That night, 9.15 was train time. After last night's party, I was in hangover mode. But when I was thinking about the train to Jaipur, I felt goose bumps all over. Jaipur, here I am, coming! Rohit looked calm, not much excited about the vacation. I decided to pack my bags after lunch as I was very lazy in all these matters. Rohit had already packed everything.

I wanted to shout, play music, but after seeing Rohit's condition, I somehow controlled myself. 'Rahul, I am going for a walk and will meet you in canteen for lunch at 12.30,' Rohit said to me. I think he needed space; I didn't want to ask him where he was going, but I guess he was going to meet Rashmi. As soon as he left the room, I started his desktop and played my Sufi songs. I love Sufi songs; Sufi music has the healing power. I lay down and closed my eyes and started listening to Sufi songs. I checked the time; it was 12.15. It was time to go for lunch, as Rohit told me that he would come directly to the canteen. After our last lunch for the semester, we both returned to F26. I was seeing major changes in Rohit. He was not talking much, always in himself. Maybe because of Uncle's incident. I wanted to ask him, but then I ignored the situation. I thought once we reached Jaipur and stayed there for a month, he would be fine.

Eight thirty p.m.: We reached the Ahmedabad Central Railway Station, and I checked the chart. Platform No. 8: Ahmedabad–Jaipur Express - On Time. Thank God the train was on time. In India if the train was on time, it was surprising news. By 9.35 the train started (twenty minutes late). If I had the power to fast-forward time, I would do it by twelve hours. I was very much excited for Jaipur. My family, my friends were waiting for us. Rohit and I both had the upper berth in coach S1. Rohit slept immediately, but I was not getting sleepy. I wanted to write something, but all were sleeping, so I couldn't switch on the light. I decide to come to the main gate of the bogie, which was the only place I can write.

> Hai Dhuva ye sham to kya baat hai,
> Hai Andhrere ye raat to kya baat hai,
> Aayege ek din Roshni inhe aandhero ko cherte huvi,
> abhe rutha hai ye naseeba to kya baat hai!

Finally at 2 a.m., I returned to my seat for sleep! But my mind was running at 120 kilometres per hour. I was thinking what I would do in this one-month vacation. I give up again and came to the main gate and started writing. I love train journey: so many strangers you would meet, so much fun it has. Finally, at night, 10.20 p.m., we reached the Jaipur. The Pink City. I never had this kind of feeling which I was feeling that time after reaching Jaipur. I took a big breath as if I wanted to feel whole Jaipur's fragrance. Now I realize, when you were far from your motherland and return to it after a long time, how it feels. As soon as we came out of the station, I saw Bunty was waiting for us. Bunty was our classmate till twelfth. He was typical Baniya. His father was running a sweet shop which was very famous in Jaipur. He was ultra-rich guy. Bunty came in his new Maruti Esteem. He was a good guy but always wanted to show off. From the station, our home is ten kilometres, hardly twenty minutes in a car. I sat at the front seat. Rohit sat at the back. Bunty was more excited than us. I wanted to meet my mom and sister as soon as possible. Finally, I was in my city. Near to 11 p.m., we reached our village, Nav-Jivan, where I saw my mom and Rohit's mom were waiting for us. I bent myself to touch my mother feet for her blessing and then Rohit's mom. I enquired about Uncle's health; he was fine and recovering, Aunty told to us. I returned to my home; my sister, Romi, and my father both were waiting for me. I was feeling so good. As soon as I entered, my sister, Romi, started crying while hugging me. Me and my father didn't have much friendly relation; it is same as Indian father and son. I never showed my love for him; neither does he. Maybe this is what Indian male nature is.

I was tired, so after some time, I decide to sleep. We have a two-storey building, not big but have three bedrooms. At the ground floor we have the living room and kitchen, My parents' bedroom is on the ground floor. My sister's and my bedroom are on the first floor with the small terrace, which we converted into a small garden space. I felt so alive after entering my bedroom.

28 November 2002

The morning was so bright but cold! I feel so alive at home. Today I planned to go to the fort where we used to hang out. I called Bunty for my evening plans; he would be free after six in evening. After breakfast, I headed towards Rohit's house. I enter Uncle's bedroom at the first floor; Rohit was already sitting there. Uncle looked better, but on his face I was not able to see the glow. Uncle enquired about our college and our grades in the internal exam, but I could sense some kind of fear in his voice. I and Rohit came to his terrace; I ask Rohit to join in the evening with me and other friends at Fort. He didn't want to come, but after my second request, he agreed to come. At 7 p.m., I, Rohit, Bunty, and other school friends reached the Fort. Bunty came with the cool beer cans. From Fort you could see lovely Jaipur at night with lots of lights; for me it's like beautiful bride jewel with stars. I lighted my *sutta* and started having chilled Foster's; I didn't want anything more from life. If I could have one wish granted, I would ask the time to stop there and then. Alcohol is the greatest thing in the world, I believed. Once it is diluted in the human body, all pains come out. After 3 hours of party we all decided to stay at Bunty's place, He had a big bungalow. Moreover, we couldn't go home like this in this drunk state.

Everybody, including Bunty, immediately slept. I thought this was the best time to discuss with Rohit about his present state. I asked him what issue was making him so tense. Under the alcohol's influence, he immediately started crying like a small baby. I hugged him. 'I am very much tense about my father, he is not telling anything to us, but there are some business problem,' he said to me. Rohit was tense because if Uncle kept everything inside, it was not good for his health. 'Rahul, I am missing Rashmi, I love her so much. Does she have the same feeling for me?'

'I think you should tell your feeling to Rashmi, without a second thought.' He switched on Bunty's desktop and opened his Orkut account. I was feeling sleepy and not able to instruct my eye to be open. So I slept immediately.

Morning, around 6, Rohit was shaking me to get up. I was not able to open my eyes, was not able to listen to his voice. But finally, I gave up and got up. Rohit looked tense. 'What happened to you, man, why you woke me up so early! You also sleep,' I told him, but he was not allowing me to sleep. Finally, I gave up and asked him to give me five minutes to freshen up. I was not a morning person, and after waking up, I did require my own time to come into the world of senses. I returned after ten minutes from Bunty's lavish bathroom. Everybody was sleeping so peacefully.

Colour of Love Hormones

29 November 2002

At the risk of sounding like a desperate boy, I want to tell you that I could not able to erase you from my thought. You came into my life when I was least expecting any happiness. When I saw you the first time, I don't know what clicked, but from that moment, I couldn't get you out from my mind. I never knew that love would come into my life like this. Your one smile can fix a thousand problems of my life in seconds. The way you see life is pretty and simple, and I want to be part of that simple life. Whenever I am with you, I feel so relaxed and I feel you are the mirror in which I can see myself. Your touch makes me alive. Your fragrance, your eye sparks, your smile make the reason to live. Whenever you are not around, I feel an emptiness, and only your presence makes my world so beautiful. I don't know how to describe you in any language, because I believe God never created that language in which I can describe you. I don't know why I open your Orkut account so many times in a day to just see your profile pic. I don't know what is love, but if being with you is love, then I am in love with you. I love you, Rashmi. I want to grow old with you.

I was shocked to read this mail which Rohit had sent at night, 3.19 a.m., to Rashmi. I didn't know what to say. I could understand his situation. He wanted to tell all this to Rashmi, but not like this, and even I wanted him to express his love when we spoke last night, but not like this. Rohit couldn't undo this thing; somehow he was feeling to hack her account and delete this mail before she could read it, but it was not possible. 'Don't worry, Rohit, everything would be OK.' I know something was going to knock at the door after Rashmi read this mail, but we didn't have any way out. The second day of vacation and big bombs hit Rohit. Today I realize one thing: Alcohol is the best thing in the world. It makes work so easy which otherwise looks so hard to do. We decided to return to our home without even bothering to inform the rest of the gang.

I was very hungry after yesterday night's beer party. My mom and my sister prepared so many things for breakfast, which I always missed at Ahmedabad. 'Bhiya, we have your favourite dal batti and churma in lunch.' Wow, if heaven existed, then it was here. Nice breakfast followed by lunch. What else could man want? Today I decided to stay the full day at home. After breakfast, I called Rohit, but still he was not able to come out after last night's incident. 'Don't worry, let's wait for her reaction, we can't do much now.' He told me, 'Should I call her and say sorry?' I told him no, as sorry sounded like he was running away from his proposal, and if she also had same feelings, sorry would make it worst, and she might think Rohit was not man enough to handle the situation. And why should he be sorry? He was in love, and to express own feeling was not a crime. 'Don't call to her, wait some more time, she may reply.' But I know even if I would have been at Rohit's place, I would have reacted the same way as he was reacting now.

A couple of days passed, but there was no reply from her. Rohit kept checking his mail whenever he got time. When you are expecting something or wait for something, you basically want time to fly, but it then never happens.

'Did she read it? Is she angry with me? No reply means what?' This was what Rohit kept asking me!

Rohit changed. A boy who thought from the brain was now thinking from the heart. I think this is called love hormones. By seeing Rohit, I felt science was meeting with art. In my way, if I wanted to describe it, it was like the sun was meeting the earth very far at one beautiful evening.

8 December 2002

Vacation was going great for me, but Rohit was not able to enjoy. He was in constant tension. He was not joining our gang for any plan. I wish I could help him, but I couldn't do anything. I could only pray that Rashmi replied on a positive note. Today we all friends decided to go for the movie, followed by lunch, and I convinced Rohit to join. When I was about to leave home, my sister shouted, 'Bhiya, it's Rohit, phone.' I wondered why he called now anyhow; I was going there only.

'Come fast, Rashmi replied to mail.'

Before I could speak anything, he hung up the phone. I rushed to the first floor of his house, where Rohit was sitting in front of a computer. 'Sorry,' Rashmi replied to Rohit's mail. A one-liner reply.

'Hey, what does it mean? Sorry for what? Sorry because she was refusing or sorry because she doesn't like me? What the hell? Should I call her? Let's preplan our Ahmedabad ticket.'

I realized one thing that day. Love hormones have higher priority over any other hormone, and love hormones ignite other hormones! Rohit was behaving so frustratedly. 'Calm down, Rohit.'

Rashmi gave her landline number to Rohit before leaving for vacation. I didn't know why she gave the number to Rohit. Did she want Rohit to call? If Rohit didn't send this e-mail, at least he could call her without any tension, but now the situation was different. Rohit was asking me whether he should call or not. I didn't think he should call her; Rohit didn't know her family members. 'Let's wait to end our vacation, and once we reach Ahmedabad, you can ask her what she would think about you.' But as usual, Rohit was completely disagreed with me.

'I want to call her.'

I gave up and allowed him to call; my allowance was just formalities.

He finally called her. I was just looking at Rohit's facial expression.

'Hello! Ramakant bol raha hu! App kon bol rahe ho!'. A strong voice from the other side.

Rohit looked speechless for a couple of seconds. 'Uncle, Rohit here, Rashmi's friend, can I talk to her?'

'Rashmi, beta tumhara phone hai!' Uncle didn't ask anything and called Rashmi to attend the phone, which was a big relief for Rohit. 'Hello?' A beautiful voice made Rohit again alive. 'Hello, who is this?'

'Hey, Rashmi, this is Rohit. How are you?' Before he could tell her anything, her voice became wet, and she just said three words—'I am sorry'—and cut the phone.

'Should I call her again? Why she hang up the phone, and why she was crying and said "I am sorry"! What does it mean!'

Rohit was becoming restless, but I believed this was the normal feeling in love. I wanted to give him space, but at the same time, I didn't him to do some stupid act. His scream broke my thought process.

'Rahul, please tell her how much I love her!' I held him and asked him to behave like a man and wait for right time. I didn't know whether he listened to me or not.

Somehow we passed the vacation, It was only one week to go back to Ahmedabad. I didn't want to go away again from my family but couldn't help it, and on the other side, Rohit wanted to fly as soon as possible.

Melting Soul

1 January 2003

It was first day of the New Year, and our first journey of the year would start from evening. I was feeling a little sad, but somehow I managed myself. I was generally good at hiding my feelings. I don't know when and why I became like this. We would have the train at 9 p.m. Rohit and I decided that we would go in Bunty's car as we did have lots of luggage, especially lots of food items. Indian moms are a bit crazy about food items for their children. They think only in their kitchenfoodwas available and their children would not get anything outside. After mixed emotions, time has come to leave from the hometown and go back to college life to start the new semester. Anytime, our results would come.

We all gathered at our society gate. My mummy and my sister were about to cry. Rohit's dad now looked a bit OK, but I don't know. I felt he was hiding something from his family. We all hugged one another, and then my sister, my mom, and Rohit's mom broke down, started crying as if we were going on a mission to Mars. I was very bad at expressing my feelings, but I also didn't want to go away from them again, but I couldn't help it.

Rohit hugged his dad and asked him to take care; both were trying to control themselves but couldn't. Both had wet eye corners. I believe it was the most beautiful feeling in the world. I hugged my dad, my mom, and my sweet sister. I was about to cry, but I managed myself so as not to hurt my male ego. We sat in the car, and Bunty started the car, and we finally were leaving after spending a beautiful vacation.

2 January 2013

A beautiful Thursday morning. We reached Ahmedabad. Rohit looked so anxious to reach hostel very fast. I now didn't want to control his emotions. I wanted him to face Rashmi and convince her of his love. After a month of luxury, we reached F26, our territory. I already had plans to drop today's college, but Rohit didn't have any plan to drop as he had to ask so many questions to Rashmi. Rohit reached the college; his eyes searching only for Rashmi, but he couldn't find her in the classroom. After all the lectures, he came to the room with a tense face. We both decided to have our lunch at the hostel mess. Rohit looked so lost. 'Don't worry, she may not return from home still maybe Monday, she will come,' I told to Rohit.

Next day, we got ready for college. I was a bit excited to attend the first class of the new semester. As soon as we reached the class, Rashmi was already sitting at her usual first bench. Rohit joined her at the first bench, but then she changed the place and went to Shruti. I then came from my last bench to join Rohit to give him moral support. He was very restless about Rashmi's behaviour but controlled himself so as not to create any discomfort for Rashmi in the classroom. Our head of department entered the classroom with his usual attitude. 'Congratulations, class! We have just received the fax from university for the result. It is the 100 per cent.' As soon as he told this 100 per cent result, I was relieved. The result would be displayed on the notice board, but I wanted to congratulate our first three rankers, Rohit, Rashmi, Yogesh.'

I just hugged my bro Rohit; he was about to cry. Our HOD left the class; all were wishing first three rankers. Rohit was about to wish Rashmi, but she left the classroom with Shruti. We all then rushed to the notice board to look at our results. I got good marks and secured distinction in all the subjects, which is a very satisfying result for me. One benefit of having rankers as friend is, you will always secure good marks even if you just are average in the study. Rohit looked so tense even after first rank, as he wanted to wish her, wanted to tell her how much he loves her. Rohit bunk the next lecture and walked to girls' hostel to meet Rashmi. He just knocked on the door of Rashmi's room. Shruti came out and told him, 'Rashmi is very disturbed from you, please leave her alone.' Rohit asked Shruti for five minutes; he wanted to talk to Rashmi. Rashmi finally agreed and asked Shruti to leave them alone. Rohit entered the room after Shruti left. A pin-drop silence. Both didn't know where to start. Rohit gathered courage and told her, 'I love you, Rashmi. Actually, I want to tell you this long back, but I couldn't. I want to tell you this looking into your eyes, but I couldn't. I don't know when I develop this feeling for you, but it is true that I love you lots.

'Look through my eyes and you'll see yourself as best as you could be in a single soul, surrounding my being in my every moment of glee!

'Whiff through my nose, and you'll smell so far and wide as you could tell. It's your aroma to heaven through hell. That's how much in love I fell!

'Listen through my ears, and you'll hear your voice as far as you could hear. The sweet melody distant, yet so near. It's surely beyond love, and not the mere.

'Be inside my soul, and you'll feel. To the depth that you could unveil yourself, inside of me, with blooming zeal. Yourself, inside of me, so surreal!

'Be myself, you be how I prevail without you. I'm all fragile, frail. It's you, you, and you, all through the sail. It's you and only you that you entail!'

Rohit shifted closer to Rashmi; her eyes were wet, and she started crying. He held her very tightly.

'I love you, Rohit, but—!'

Rohit put his finger on her lips and said, 'I love you, my life, Rashmi. I don't want to listen any *if* and *but*. You love me, that's the only thing I want to listen, rest is irrational.' They hugged each other. It was like melting souls.

He wrapped his right hand round hers and kept his left hand on her shoulders, bringing her close to himself. She leant on him while Rohit stroked her back. Finally, their lips met. It was their first kiss. They were both lost in pure love.

Rohit and Rashmi congratulated each other for their ranks. Rohit returned after one hour. He looked so fresh. I hadn't seen Rohit smiling fully after ages. He came to me and asked me to bunk the rest of the lectures, and I agreed. We returned to F26, and he told me she accepted his proposal and he was so excited. We decided to party at night. He wanted Rashmi to join, for which we needed to do some special arrangements as at night, boys couldn't go to the girls' hostel, and neither could they come to our F26 room. 'Don't worry, Rohit, you ask Shruti and Rashmi about night party, I will arrange something.' Rohit again went to the hostel and informed Shruti and Rashmi about the evening's plan. After a big hesitation, both finally agreed, but they wanted us to join in their room. Rohit agreed without even asking me. He returned from the hostel and informed that we had to go to their rooms. 'Are you nuts? I will not come with you.'

'Please now don't spoil plan, both girls agreed after lots of requests. Now you please don't create any scene.'

Night finally arrived. Rohit and I were excited and nervous at the same time. Breaking the rules of a girls' hostel and sneaking in could be nasty if we were caught.

'If you get caught, then you at least have a valid reason. You can tell them that you're Rashmi's boyfriend. What can I say? That I'm a tharki who just came for sightseeing?'

'Keep your mouth shut, Rahul. You're speaking shit. Don't worry, nothing going to happen,' Rohit assured me.

This was the first time I was doing such a bold thing. We were standing in a dark passage near the girls' hostel which was hidden from public view. Shruti told Rohit that the warden was not around at 8 to 8.30 p.m., so it was the perfect chance for us to slip into the hostel. Rohit didn't think much about the consequences because getting into a girls' hostel was quite thrilling. It was no different for me, but my nervousness overshadowed the thrill. We were almost ready to walk towards the main gate, waiting for Shruti's green signal from afar.

'Crazy, what if we would have—?' I panicked.

'Chill, nothing can happen.'

I lit a cigarette and slowly inhaled a puff.

'Are you nuts? Why you are smoking here?' Rohit shouted to me.

'But I can't help, I am in so much tension.' Finally, after Shruti's green signal, we reached their room.

Finally, two souls met with each other. Rohit and Rashmi looked very cute together. We had already purchased the vodka with the help of our seniors. Shruti drinks sometimes, but for Rashmi, it was the first time.

I created four peg packs of vodka; for both girls I had made a very light drink, and for me and Rohit I made the little strong drink. 'Yuck, how can you drink this shit?' *Rashmi shouted at us after taking the first sip of vodka with cold drink*

'Go slow and add more cold drink if you want, you will like it after next sip.' Rohit tried to cover up. I lit my cigarette after taking both girls' permission. Rashmi looked OK now after finishing the first of her pack. I and Shruti were going very slow. Rohit and Rashmi finished their drinks so fast and wanted a second pack. Both college toppers were in a good mood after their love proposal. I wanted this time should stop here.

Shruti and Rashmi wanted to try cigarettes, which I didn't want them to do, but once girls are decided on anything, then nobody can stop them. Both of them lit the cigarettes as if they were chain smokers but couldn't inhale the one puff also. Waste of two cigarettes. Shruti was almost down after three packs of vodka. Rohit and I had finished two strong packs each Rashmi was about to finish three packs and she suddenly started crying. I felt a little uncomfortable, as Shruti already slept and I didn't want to be the spectator of their upcoming love session. I left the room and somehow managed to come to the terrace of the girls' hostel, where nobody could catch me at this late-night time.

Rohit hugged Rashmi very tightly and kissed her very passionately. They were in a deep ocean of love. Rohit switched off the light, which I could see from the terrace. In the girls' hostel, each block had two rooms: one very small living room and one mid-size bedroom with two single beds and, in front of the beds, a single almira. Shruti was sleeping in the living room. Rohit lifted Rashmi in his arms and went inside the room. Rashmi was feeling shy, not able to open the eyes also. Rohit started kissing very madly. Rashmi too was kissing Rohit passionately. Rohit pulled Rashmi's T-shirt and started off with kissing her neck. Rashmi moaned in pleasure. There were no dim lights, flower petals on the bed, scented candles around them, but they were experiencing lovemaking for the first time, which made it all the more special.

The cold air from window was showing its effects on Rohit. He was so close to her that he could smell her hair, which was so exotic. He inched closer to her and turned her face to the wall. He started rubbing her back and kissing her back madly. Rashmi moaned each time when Rohit bite her back. She gave a mischievous smile and pushed Rohit on the bed. She moved closer to him and started kissing him all over his body. 'Rashmi, you look so beautiful and sexy. You are mine.' Rohit teased her while sliding his hands inside her top.

'Rohit, go slowly.'

'I am not going anywhere.'

'Sometimes you behave like a small kid who bites his own tongue in the excitement of eating his own chocolate. But you look so sexy when you are in a romantic mood,' Rashmi whispered, rolling her fingers on his chest and gently moving it downwards. Meanwhile, Rohit removed her bra with his hand. She had a satisfied look on her face. At the same time she knew it was just the beginning of their love making session. She could see the affection and care in Rohit eyes, Something which Rashmi dreamt of seeing in his partner's. Rohit took the ice cubes from the glass of vine and rolled it all over her back. he let out a low moan, tearing off Rohit's clothes and reversing their positions. She locked Rohit by crossing her leg to his body and asked him to take charge. Her mesmerizing voice aroused him. She scratched her nails on his back like a hungry tigress. Rohit searched for the condom which he had secretly hidden inside his jeans. He hurried, tried to open the packet, but for some reason, it couldn't open. Rashmi started laughing. Finally, he succeeded in opening the packet. Rohit sealed her mouth by giving a kiss which turned into a passionate French kiss. Rashmi had reached the peak of sexual arousal. Finally, Rohit was completely inside her, and a drop of tear rolled down Rashmi's eyes. Rohit kissed her tears.

Eventually, pain dissolved, and they were into the deep ocean of love. Eventually, pain dissolved, and they were left with a strange and mildly pleasurable sense of conquest. It was the world of romance, and they just longed for more and more. They had never known such pleasure and satisfaction. Rashmi's heartbeat increased, and she lifted herself and moaned uncontrollably. Both reach their satisfaction almost the same time.

After an hour finally both got up and got dressed. They came out of a room with smiles on their faces; they hugged each other and kissed again. Rohit was searching for me, which I could see from the terrace. I signed for him to come to the room directly. Rohit looked complete today.

New Colour of Life

It was Rashmi's birthday on June 16. Rohit had planned a big surprise for her. They both had decided to go for the movie *Chalte Chalte* in the drive-in cinema after a Kankaria Lake visit. They asked me and Shruti to join, but we wanted them to celebrate special moments. Second-sem exams were at the corner, but it was Rashmi's birthday, and it was very special as it was the first birrthday of Rashmiafter they had accepted each other. The only problem was, the girl's hostel wouldn't allow anybody to come after 9 at night, and if anybody was missing after that time, immediately the hostel warden would call the respective girl's parents. But Shruti had planned that Shruti immediately switched off the lights of their room after mess dinner and would tell the hostel warden that Rashmi was not well and that because of that she couldn't come for dinner as well. By this lie, at least the hostel warden wouldn't come for attendance in their room, but this was one risk, in case the warden did come. But Shruti was confident that she could handle the situation and it wouldn't create any mess.

At 15 June, Rohit had purchased the Nokia 6610 colour mobile for Rashmi as a birthday surprise and one for himself, which was less costly than Rashmi's phone. They both left the hostel at 3 p.m. And directly took an auto to go to Kankaria Lake, which was a famous hangout spot of Ahmedabad. Rashmi was wearing a red salwar kameez suit, in which she was looking very beautiful with loose hair touching her shoulder, with elegant brass earrings and matching glass Bengals, which sounded like sweet birds twitting from afar when she walked. She hardly wore any make-up except the kajal and very light pink-coloured lipstick, but her simple aura made her more beautiful. She was looking like a beautiful angel. Around 4 they reached the Kankaria and sat inside the garden. They both were very happy with each other. After spending some time in the garden, both had decided to rent a boat. Both were paddling the boat, holding each other's hands. In the far distance, it was about sunset. It was a very beautiful evening, where two souls were completely lost in each other during sunset. The sky had a blaze of colours oranges, pearly pinks, vibrant purples because of the sunset. The misty clouds flashed bright red and orange behind the black summit. The lake turned into a pattern of golden streaks. Both had returned to Kankaria base after one hour of boating. After the romantic ride, they headed towards the drive-in theatre.

At the drive-in, they were holding each other's hands while watching the romantic movie *Chalte Chalte*. In the interval, it was time for Rohit's surprise. He asked Rashmi not to go anywhere and went to meet the drive-in theatre manager. Soon he came with popcorns and cold drinks in his hand. Rashmi asked him why he took so much time to get popcorn, but Rohit just passed a smile. Before the movie started, a beautiful slide covered the screen.

'Rashmi, you are my life. You came into my life like God's blessing. You filled my life with so much love that now I can't imagine my life without you. You are the oxygen of my life. You made me complete. I want to grow old with you. I want to pass each day of my life with you. I can't promise you any big things, but I promise you that I'll fill each of your days with lots of smiles. I promise you that I am not behind or ahead of you, but I am always and will be always with you in each phase of our lives, holding your hand very tightly. I want to pass all of my life's moments with you only. You are a blessing to me, you are my angel. Whenever I am with you, I feel so complete. Please be my angel and guide always. I love you, Rashmi, so much. Please marry me.' After thirty seconds of flashing this message, a spotlight came to both of them. The crowd was cheering for them. Rashmi was not able to control her emotion and broke into tears of excitement and happiness. Both hugged each other very tightly. It was the perfect moment. Soon the movie started, but Rohit and Rashmi were lost in each other. Rashmi came forward and landed a passionate kiss on Rohit in the dark. They came to their sense after a few minutes. The movie was about to end. It was time for Rohit's next surprise, Rashmi's birthday gift, the mobile. But he wanted to be surprised for Rashmi. He silently kept the mobile in Rashmi's purse. After the movie, both had a wonderful candlelight dinner. They took an auto from there and started towards the hostel, where Rashmi had to enter secretly. While returning, they were looking at each other as if they had met each other after ages. Soon the auto stopped at the girls' hostel gate. As per plan, Shruti was waiting near the main gate at 10 p.m.; she already gave a bribe to the gatekeeper. Rashmi silently went inside the hostel and then to her room. Before she could speak anything, Shruti bombarded her with lots of questions. Rashmi was blushing. Rashmi started narrating each special moment to Shruti. Here, Rohit returned to our room, where I was waiting for him. As soon as he entered, he hugged me tightly and was telling me that today was the best day of his life.

It was about to 12, time to reveal Rohit's next surprise. He took out his new phone and called Shruti's mobile, which he secretly kept inside Rashmi's purse. It was ringing. Both Shruti and Rashmi were shocked at where the ring was coming from. Finally, from the sound, Rashmi was able to find the mobile from her purse. On the screen, it was written 'Rohit'. She picked up the phone.

'Thank you so much, Rashmi, for accepting me as your partner in life journey. Today was the best day of my life. I love you, Rashmi. It is a small gift from me to my love. I love you, Rashmi.' And then he hung up the phone. Rashmi didn't know how to react, and again she was lost in emotion. Shruti hugged her.

It was exam time, but this time we all studied very hard, and by that time we had become a gang of four. Again I was feeling pressure, but Rohit and Rashmi were looking so confident as usual. This time all the faculty had high hopes for Rohit and Rashmi to top the exams again with higher percentage compared to first sem. I too had hopes for both Rohit and Rashmi, as this time there was no unexpected tension present in between exams, and moreover, both were in a relationship, which made Rohit and Rashmi more confident. Again ten days and five papers. Two days to go before the exams. Rohit and I were studying at our room at F26. Rohit suddenly stopped studying and told me that he wanted to inform his parents about Rashmi in the coming vacation. I thought it was very early to inform Uncle and

Aunty. I didn't want to give any gyan this time to Rohit, as I was too nervous about the exams.

Finally, exams got over. This time, because of Rohit, we had planned our trip to Jaipur a week after the exams, as Rashmi and Rohit wanted to spend time together. Shruti had left for her hometown. I also wanted to go to Jaipur as soon as possible, but because of Rohit I also had to stay. Rohit and Rashmi decided to visit Mount Abu for three days, but I didn't want to travel anywhere except Jaipur, and moreover, I didn't want to *kabab mein haddi* between the love couple. After one day, they both boarded the state bus to Mount Abu. From Ahmedabad, it was near-to-six–or–seven-hour journey. I dropped off both of them and came back to the hostel. I had a mixed feeling for them, as it was the first time they were going out as a couple and was a little scared for the coming time.

Present Time

Tuesday, October 28, 2008

Around 5 a.m. a surgeon has come to the hospital for Rohit's surgery. A nurse informed me to sign some of the legal documents for operation. I am in a dilemma whether to inform Rohit's parents or not, as Uncle have a heart issue. After signing all the required documents, I decide to visit the doctor. I enter into Mr Mehta's chamber to discuss Rohit's condition. The doctor looks very calm and explains to me that it was a major accident, and because of head injury, there was internal bleeding, and they need to perform the operation immediately to avoid any life-threatening risk. I understand everything and I ask the simple question, what is the chance of success? The doctor is stunned by my direct question, and with a deep breath, he informs me it is fifty-fifty, and even after a successful operation, there could be a chance that the patient may go into a coma. I stand still there, and he leaves his chamber for operation. I don't know how to react. I notice there is something wet around my eyes corner. I break down here and start crying like a small baby. I want my friend to be back. I want to undo the last six hours of Rohit's life. I somehow manage myself and decide to inform at least my parents. I am waiting for morning so that I can inform my parents.

Suddenly I am feeling so helpless. I realize one thing today: nothing is permanent in the world. Nobody knows what would be there in next moment of life. Just a few hours back, Rohit and I were enjoying drinks at his favourite place, and now I am here in this hospital. Suddenly my mind asks me to inform Priya. I immediately call her, but her number is switched off. I am feeling more nervous. I was correlating Rohit and Priya's last conversation. He was tense when he came after talking to Priya, and she was also crying. Did they fight? Did Priya tell anything to Rohit? If I dropped him off at home, then what would be a reason to again go by bike? All these questions are bombarding my mind. First I want to know which place Rohit met with an accident. I start walking to reception to enquire who brought Rohit to the hospital. The receptionist informs me that somebody called an ambulance from Airport Road, and their ambulance brought Rohit here. I am totally confused. Why the hell did Rohit go to Airport Road so late? I am not able to join a clue. I again try Priya's number, but it is coming as switched off.

Morning, 7 a.m. Still doctors is inside operation theatre. I call my parents to inform them about Rohit. My father picks up the phone. I tell him everything; he is clueless now. I ask him whether we should inform Rohit's parents or not. My father tells me we should inform Rohit's family, and he tells not to worry much; he will call me again after informing their family. My head is spinning. I again decide to have coffee and Disprin. 'Rohit Home' is flashing on my mobile; this means my father has informed them about Rohit. I gather courage and pick up the phone. As soon as I pick up the phone, Uncle starts crying and asks me about Rohit's condition. 'Don't worry, Uncle, everything will be all right. Rohit is inside operation theatre.' He breaks down completely after hearing that his son is inside operation theatre, and the phone gets disconnected. I call my father immediately, as I am worried about Uncle's heart issue. My father is with Uncle only and tells me that they all are coming to Bangalore on the next flight.

Still same question pops up in my mind: what would be the reason for Rohit to go to Airport so late? And why is Priya's number switched off. I am now waiting for doctors to finish the operation successfully. It is 10 a.m., and still operation is running; with every passing minute I am losing my nerves. 'Hello.' I hear a sudden voice from the back. It is Doctor Mehta. 'Come to my chamber.' I am continuously praying for good news. As soon as we enter his chamber, he tells me the operation is successful. 'It requires some hours for Rohit to come to his senses. Till that, we have to keep him inside the ICU only under continuous observation.' I am not able to control my tears in front of Mr Mehta.

'Thank you lot, sir. You have saved my friend's life. Thank you so much.' I hug Mr Mehta; he also reciprocates. Sometimes a simple hug gives you lots of strength. I immediately call Rohit's home to inform them about the operation. 'Uncle, Rohit is out of any risks, his operation is successful,' I inform Rohit's father.

'Thank you, beta, for being with him always, we will be there by evening,' Uncle informs me. Now I feel a bit relaxed.

Around evening, 5 p.m., Rohit's parents and my father arrive at the hospital. Uncle and Aunty are looking so tense, and they want to meet Rohit. I inform a nurse that they are Rohit's parents and want to see his son. Nurse instructs them about ICU procedure and then allows them one by one to visit Rohit. I decide to visit the room and get all the necessary stuff for the night. I again try Priya's number and try to reach her, but result is in vain; her number is switched off. Now I highly suspect that there is something big that happened between Rohit and Priya.

In between, I forgot to call Shruti. I didn't check my mobile till now. Shruti had called me more than twenty times and dropped twelve messages. 'Don't talk to me, I am worried, even I went to your house, you and Rohit are not in the house. I called Rohit and Priya phones, both are not reachable. I am so worried.' She starts crying.

I tell her to control herself and then ask her to be ready. 'I am coming to pick you up.' Within half an hour, I reach Shruti's PG and take her to our home. I tell her entire story, and she is shocked. I ask her to order some food, as I didn't have anything, and I need to go to the hospital soon, so I will take something for dinner for everybody. Shruti asks me to sleep for some time; meanwhile, she will arrange everything. Shruti is my nervous system; without her, I can't do anything. Now I can correlate Rohit's situation.

First Problem of Life to Face Alone

June 2004

It was fourth-semester exam time, and till now nobody was able to overtake Rohit. He was three-time topper, and Rashmi always secured second rank. So people stopped checking first two places, as they were always secured by Rohit and Rashmi. It was only one semester to go for campus recruitment, and all the faculty had high hopes for Rohit and Rashmi. Even now, the faculty knows about Rohit and Rashmi's relationship. They were the lovely couple who always supported each other. This would be last semester in which we could go home for vacation, as during fifth semester's vacation, campus recruitments would start. Till third semester, I also secured 78 per cent aggregate and was hoping for some good, decent MNC campus selection.

This time we had booked Jaipur tickets for 2 July, which was one day after the exams were completed. In one spare day, we had decided to party. Morning, we decided to have a great lunch in one of the big fat Gujarati restaurants. Gang of 4. That was the name of our group, Rohit, Rashmi, Rahul, and Shruti. People thought that I and Shruti were a couple like Rohit and Rashmi, but I had never seen Shruti like that, but sometimes I felt that Shruti liked me. After lunch, we had planned to visit the Akashrdham Temple. It took one hour for us to reach the temple. I saw Rashmi and Rohit from afar; they looked very beautiful with each other. I prayed to god for their coming life and prayed that their family members would accept one another without much tension. After a wonderful day out, we had returned to the hostel at night and started packing our luggage. Two years back we were waiting for our entrance exam results, and now this was the end of the fourth semester. One semester to go for placement. Rohit and I had decided that we would have a blast this vacation, as this would be the last official vacation.

First of July, Ahmedabad–Jaipur train. Rohit called Rashmi, who already left in the morning, to inform her that our train was on time. Second July, by night, we had reached Jaipur. That time, I was feeling a little low as we didn't know where we could place. Whether Rohit and I could get into same campus company or not. Maybe this was the last time we would be together for such a long time. Rohit and I studied together till date, so such thought made my nervous system go down. But then I decided not to think much. As soon as we had reached Jaipur, Rohit called Rashmi to inform her that we had arrived, but she didn't pick up the phone. He tried twice, but same result. I told him not to call her too much, as her father didn't know that she had a mobile and that, too, Rohit gifted her. I told Rohit that she would call once she checked his missed calls. I slept immediately after reaching home as I was too tired. In the morning, my sister was shouting to me that Rohit Bhiya had come down and was asking for me. I thought now what the problem was. I went down; Rohit asked me to come out. I came to the society garden. Rohit was looking very tense. 'What happened now?' I asked Rohit.

'Yar, I called Rashmi fifteen times today morning, and Rashmi has not called back and not replied to any of my messages, and now her phone is switched off.'

I almost shouted at him, 'Why the hell you called her so many times?'

But in turn he shouted at me and immediately called Rashmi's landline number. After a long ring, Rashmi's father picked up the phone. 'Uncle, Rohit this side, can I talk to Rashmi?'

'Rohit, from now onwards, don't call Rashmi. Otherwise, I will complain to your parents and your college faculty also.' And he hang up the phone.

My fear had come true. When Rashmi's parents didn't know about the mobile phone which Rohit had gifted to Rashmi, why the hell did Rohit call her so many times? But now I had to handle Rohit for his own mistake. He became so restless; even if I were there at his place, I would have reacted in the same manner which he was doing that time. 'Don't worry now, you don't call, Rashmi is a smart girl, she will handle it. Wait for her call now.' And then I went to my home. I sensed the worst vacation. I wanted to scold Rohit for his stupidity, but I couldn't. Four days passed, but there was no call from Rashmi. Day by day, Rohit's tensions were increasing. Rohit just wanted to listen to the voice of Rashmi, whether she was fine or not. What could be her situation? Rohit desperately wanted to talk with Rashmi. I got one idea; my sister could call Rashmi's landline number and introduce her as Shruti, then Uncle wouldn't doubt, and once she would come to the phone line, Rohit would talk. But to execute this plan, I had to tell the truth to my sister. Rohit agreed to this plan, and we took a promise from my sister that she wouldn't tell anything about Rashmi to anybody. She agreed. We would call her tomorrow afternoon so that her father would have left home for work.

Next morning, we called Rashmi's landline number; we were expecting that Rashmi would pick up. But as per Murphy's Law, Aunty picked up the phone. But as per plan, my sister introduced herself as Shruti and asked for Rashmi. After initial investigations, Aunty gave the phone to Rashmi. As soon as Rashmi came on the phone line, Rohit took the phone. 'Sorry, Rashmi, for that day, I was tense, that's why I called you so many times. What Uncle has told? How are you?' He was not allowing Rashmi to talk only.

'Rohit, please don't call, we will talk once we will be at Ahmedabad.' And she hung up the call. After which, Rohit became more tense.

'Now, we can't do much, Rohit, let us wait for vacation to be over.'

From that day onwards, Rohit again became silent. When we least expect anything, life comes up with big unwanted surprises.

First Heartbreak.

2 August 2004

We had not enjoyed our last vacation as planned because of the tension. In the morning, we had reached the Ahmedabad station and then immediately booked the auto for the college. Rashmi also returned on the same date, and by this time she would have reached the hostel also. Rohit called her on her mobile, but it was switched off, which increased Rohit's tension. After one hour we reached the hostel. Rohit handed his luggage to me and started walking towards the girls' hostel to meet Rashmi. I was shocked to see Rohit's restlessness. But then I thought that if I would have been in his place, I would have behaved the same way. I returned to our room with lots of luggage. After ten minutes, Rohit returned to the room. 'Did you meet Rashmi?' I asked him.

'I met Shruti, and she informed me that Rashmi will come after three days, and Rashmi informed her that I should not call her till she will be back.' Rohit's face became full dull, but he couldn't do much until waiting for Rashmi to join the college.

Next morning, I got up, but Rohit refused to come for college. I told him that nothing could happen if he lost faith like this. But he told me he first wanted to talk to Rashmi. I also thought to give him some space, and I left the hostel to attend the first class of the fifth semester. As soon as I entered the class, Shruti called me and asked me to sit with her. After the first lecture, Shruti asked me to bunk the rest of the lectures as she wanted to talk with me regarding Rashmi and Rohit. We came to the canteen. Shruti asked me about the incident. I briefly described what had happened. She told that Rashmi's father was very angry at Rashmi and Rohit, and he is searching a well-settled boy for Rashmi. I asked who told her all these to her. She told me Rashmi called her after three days from that incident and she was very tense. She told me that her father was very strict and nobody could speak a word against him. She was very scared. He took the promise that she would never talk to Rohit, and on that basis only, he agreed to send Rashmi back to finish the course. I became very cold after hearing Shruti talk. She told me that I should not inform Rohit about our discussion, and once Rashmi would come, she only would talk to Rohit.

I returned to the room after meeting with Shruti. Rohit was totally unaware of the tension which would knock on the door after three days. I was totally confused whether to inform Rohit about what had happened with Rashmi or not. Anyhow, after three days he would get to know, so why give him tension now? So I kept quiet. Rohit was so restless that he even refused to have dinner. But then after so much of my insistence, he agreed to come for dinner.

I was feeling guilty by not informing the Rohit, but if I informed him what I and Shruti had discussed, then I don't know how he would react. But then I had decided to tell him the truth. I had told him everything that Shruti had told to me. After this, he became more restless, but then I made him understand that if both loved each other, then with peace of mind, both would get their way out. But he was not convinced with any of my arguments. Next morning, also he wanted to bunk the classes, but then I forcefully dragged him to the classroom. All day he was lost; physically he was in class but mentally very tense. He was waiting for Rashmi to come so that he could discuss everything and clear her doubts, if any she had. I had never seen Rohit so silent, not even two years before, when Uncle got a first stroke. He was looking so dull. Everybody was asking me the reason, as Rohit stopped communication with the class. Now Rohit was waiting for the third day, when Rashmi was supposed to join the college.

Next morning, Rohit got up very early—I can say he had not slept that night—and got ready and started walking towards the girls' hostel. As soon as he entered the visitors' area, he met Shruti. Shruti informed him that Rashmi had come and would join college that day. Rohit wanted to meet Rashmi that time only. He asked Shruti to please inform Rashmi that he was waiting for her, but Shruti told him that it would better if he met her at the college. Rohit didn't have any choice and returned to the room with a very dull face. Anyhow, now he had to wait till class started. At 9 a.m., we both had reached the class. Rohit's eyes were continuously searching for Rashmi, but it was in vain. She had not come yet. We all settled down as HOD Ranganath entered the class. Behind the HOD, Rashmi arrived. She greeted HOD and took permission to enter the classroom. Now we all had fixed position in the class. Rohit's next seat was empty where Rashmi was seated till date, but then she ignored Rohit completely and sat next to Shruti. I and Rohit both were clueless but then not in a position to react to anything. 'Good morning, class, welcome to the fifth semester, last semester to study. At the end of this semester, almost all big company would come to hire you and give the project for your sixth semester. So please put the paddle and win the medal. By the way, congratulation to Rohit and Rashmi for their ranks in fourth semester. Nobody was expecting the result would come in this way. Others student can see their result on the notice board. Once again, congratulations to both of you, and all the best to class.' As soon as HOD exited, the class all were congratulating Rohit and Rashmi. Rohit immediately went to Shruti's seat and congratulated Rashmi; she in turn congratulated him, but that spark was missing. Within a minute, Rashmi left the class. Rohit also left the class to talk to Rashmi.

'Rohit, please don't follow me.' Rohit asked her to give him five minutes to talk, which she refused and left Rohit.

Rohit bunked the remaining classes. I didn't understand how to tackle this situation. I asked Shruti to talk to Rashmi. After the college, when I returned to the room, Rohit was full high and had finished four bottles of beer. I was shocked and screamed at Rohit for his behaviour, but rather than replying anything, he handed his mobile phone to me. There was a message from Rashmi.

> Rohit, Please forgive me. From now onwards we both has to focus on our coming future. I couldn't continue our relationship. I was not ready that time also when you proposed me, but I just said yes because of your good nature. But I don't have any feeling for you. It's better that we both should focus on our placement and prove our important to our parents. I always respect you but I don't have feeling for you. Please don't try to follow me or call me, otherwise I have to make complaints to the college authority. Wish you best of luck in your future.

What the fuck! I was speechless after reading the message from Rashmi. I didn't know how to react and what to tell Rohit. Did she really mean what she sent, or was it just a side effect of Uncle's emotional blackmail? If she was not ready, she could have told Rohit directly Why the hell was she behaving like this? My mind was surrounded with millions of questions. There were knocks at the door. I thought, *Who the hell came this time?* As soon as I opened the door, the hostel room cleaner boy was standing with mobile in hand. 'Sir, ye Rashmi Madam ne diya hai, Rohit Sir ko dene ko.' She returned the mobile which Rohit gave her. I almost lost control. I wanted to shout at Rashmi, but I couldn't do that. Rohit broke down completely. I wanted to go to Rashmi's room and ask her why she was behaving like this, but at this point, I should be by Rohit, as he completely broke down.

Bad Times Knock at the Door

6 August 2004

I didn't get any sleep after last day's incident. Rohit was still sleeping because of excess alcohol. I gathered courage and shook Rohit to wake him up. I realized that Rohit had a very high fever. I immediately took Rohit to the doctor. He gave him medicine and asked him to rest. But I only knew how a person could rest when his own life has turned back from him. I gave Rohit medicine and decided to go to the class and talk to Rashmi personally. As soon as I entered the class, I saw Rashmi was sitting with Shruti. I went to Shruti's seat and asked Rashmi to come out for two minutes. She came out with Shruti. Without worrying much about Shruti's presence, I asked Rashmi about her behaviour towards Rohit.

'See, Rahul, If you want to talk regarding Rohit, I don't have time. I do not like him and I told him the truth. Why you were taking his side and talking to me? That matter was over, and I don't want to give any clarification to anybody.' She left the place and went inside the classroom. I was standing shocked as if somebody had cut my main nerves. She didn't even bother to talk or even ask about Rohit. Rather than attending the class, I had come back to our room.

Friday. Black Friday. Rohit's fever was not coming down. He broke completely. I had to stay with him. I went to the mess to ask the in charge to prepare some light lunch for Rohit. I gave him the medicine which the doctor suggested for him By afternoon the fever was gone, but the spark was missing from Rohit's face. Rohit slept after lunch, so I decided to go meet Rashmi. I went to the girls' hostel and asked the warden to call Rashmi. After five minutes of wait, Rashmi came down. 'Rashmi, I need to talk to you. Can we go to college garden?' She refused and asked me to tell her whatever I wanted to tell her there only. 'Rohit broke completely, he needs you. Please talk to him.' I literally begged her, but there was no sign of worries on Rashmi's face.

'Rahul, please take care of Rohit. I already told him that I couldn't continue this relation.' She left after telling me. I was so shocked. How could someone be so selfish? At least on the human ground she could talk to Rohit. All my efforts were in vain. I was directionless. With a heavy heart, I came to our room. Rohit was still sleeping because of the medicine's effect, but I could see his eyes were swelled up.

I decided to go to college once Rohit would recover. Saturday, we both stayed at room only. He didn't have any fever, but he became so weak. Somehow we passed Saturday, but from inside I broke completely. He trusted Rashmi so much and suddenly she changed her behaviour; that's not fair. We had a college fest; Rohit was supposed to take part in the technical discussion, but he didn't have the strength. I wanted him to focus somewhere else so that he could recover fast. I insisted for him not to drop out from the fest; finally, he agreed. That morning, we reached our college auditorium, where ten people were selected from different colleges. From our college, Rohit and Rashmi were selected. Rohit somehow controlled his emotion as all the professors and dignitaries were present. He sat next to Rashmi. They both were representing our college. Rashmi was ignoring him by not looking at him at all. Every team was given ten minutes to discuss topics given by judges. Every other college team spoke about the current technology; our college's turn was last. Rohit stood up with Rashmi and started discussing. Both were taking the discussion at the right direction. Both were so confident and going like smooth flow. At the end of the discussion, judges announced the result. It was our college that won the first prize. Rohit congratulated Rashmi and did shake her hands. Rohit's eyes were asking so many questions to Rashmi. She was continuously ignoring eye contact with Rohit. They won the trophy; a photographer was taking their pictures. Both were looking a perfect couple. If both gave support to each other, nobody could beat them. Both were not complete with each other. After the event Rashmi left.

'Rohit, stop drinking!' I screamed at him. After Rashmi broke up with him, it was a daily affair for him. Slowly, slowly everybody noticed a change in Rohit. Now he frequently bunked the classes. Not concentrating on the study. He stopped visiting the library for study. Only thing he was doing was to attend the classes. Somehow we had given the first internal exam. By this time, everybody knew that both Rohit and Rashmi broke up with each other.

The result was announced and was shocking to everybody. This time Rashmi was first rank and Rohit dropped from first to nowhere. He just scored 70 per cent. I scored 82 per cent, first time I had scored more than 80 per cent, but I was feeling very bad for Rohit. Rashmi moved on, but Rohit was not able to come out. It was major drop for Rohit. Next morning, the HOD arranged for a meeting with Rohit. He had to work hard again as he was the hope for the college for first rank in university After this incident also, Rashmi did not initiate anything. Daily I guided Rohit, but it didn't have any impact on him.

Within the month, our second internal was around the corner. Rohit lost touch from everywhere. He was spoiling his life, and I was not able to save him. He became a full drinker and smoker. His daily schedule was to attend the class and then at night drink beer. I decided that I would talk to Shruti and do something. I couldn't sit quietly like this. I wanted Rohit to come up again and prove himself. That morning, I bunked the class and asked Shruti to join me. Shruti agreed. I discussed everything with Shruti and asked her to talk to Rashmi. Finally, I and Shruti arranged for a meeting with Rashmi without Rohit's knowledge.

Rashmi, Shruti, and I met at Kankaria Lake, where Rohit and Rashmi had first dated. 'Rashmi can't you see Rohit's condition? You both were so happy with each other, after fourth-sem vacation incident, you completely stopped talking to Rohit. I do understand your problem, but please try to think from Rohit's point of view.'

She broke down completely and started crying in front of us. Shruti was consoling her, but I asked Shruti not to stop her from crying. Sometimes it is good to cry and take out frustration. 'I love Rohit very much, but my father took the promise that I would never talk to him.'

Once Rashmi settled down, I explained that there would many such obstacles coming in future; both had to support each other. 'If you do not give him support now, he would break completely and lose in life. Love not only means to achieve but to support each other in hard times,' I explained to Rashmi. 'Don't go against your parents, but slowly explain to your parents that Rohit is the only one with whom you will be happy. Once you both get a good job, that time you can explain to your parents.'

Finally, Rashmi agreed after a long discussion. I took a relieved breath that night.

Next morning, Rashmi came to class and sat next to Rohit. I and Shruti were seeing this from afar. There was a special glow on Rohit's face after ages. After all the classes, Rashmi asked Rohit to come with her to the college garden. 'I am sorry, Rohit.' Rohit kept his finger at Rashmi's lips, not to speak a single word. Both broke down completely and started crying. They didn't utter a single word, but they ended the confusion with a simple hug. That night, I got my friend back. Thanks to Shruti, who made this meeting. From next day, Rohit started studying in the library for the second internal. Finally, our second internal was over, and we decided to celebrate.

Placements Time!
Beginning of New Life!

After Rohit and Rashmi patched up, Rohit scored 92 per cent in the internals exam. We were ready for the final exam, and in the fifth-sem vacation we had campus recruitments. This was the day for which we had waited for two years. Our final exam went well.

Jan 3, 2005. First company! Morning, 8 a.m., ABS Soft Corps. ABS Soft Corps was famous to select only toppers and people who had the good presence of mind to solve a complex problem. We were so nervous. We all dressed up in business formals. I was not at all comfortable but had to stick with business attire. Morning, 8.30, we were gathered to our auditorium, where ABS Soft Corps would give the presentation about the company and tell us about the selection process. From our seniors' batch, five people were selected for ABS. Last night we already took the session from our seniors who were selected last year. Around 9 a.m., ABS Corps HR entered the auditorium and greeted us and started the presentation.

He introduced himself as Aakash Jain, HR and recruitment manager. He was in his early 40s. I was sitting at third-row corner seat, from where I could see Rohit and Rashmi, who sat at second row, holding each other's hands. They were looking perfect and confident, but I was so tense, as if this could be the last company that came for campus selection. Aakash took forty-five minutes to give an overview of the company. After which he told us that there would be five rounds.

1. Written Round
2. Group Discussion Round
3. Technical Round
4. One-to-One Round with Technical Manager
5. HR Round

I already accepted that I could not even clear two rounds. Immediately after Aakash finished the presentation, we moved to our exam hall for the written round. It was a one-hour round. We were waiting for the first round's result. Soon one person from ABS came with the result; he was announcing the names. My heartbeat was increasing with each name he spelled out. After the tenth name, he announced Rohit's name, followed by Rashmi's name. He announced almost forty names of the different branches, and then I heard my name. I took a relieved breath. After which we had divided into teams of ten people for group discussion round. I was very confident about this round to clear. Rohit was in a different team, and I and Rashmi were in the same team. Now that was called fate. In group discussion, you have to prove your point on top of others but as Rashmi was in my team, I felt a bit reluctant. The topic given to us was 'education knowledge v/s presence of mind'. I was in favour of presence of mind being always greater over educational knowledge, but Rashmi was in favour of education knowledge. Literally, we had divided into two teams. There were four people, including Rashmi, who were supporting education knowledge, and we team of six were arguing on presence of mind. I found it difficult to argue with Rashmi not because she was good but because she was Rohit's girlfriend. But then somehow I managed to give my best that time. After fifteen minutes of discussion, HR asked us to wait for the result. 'I am sorry, Rashmi, as this is just discussion, nothing personal,' I explained to her. Before I finished with Rashmi, Rohit arrived from his GD round. He looked so confident.

We needed a break, as we were tense, so Rohit and I came out for a smoke. He asked me about GD round. I explained what at all happened in GD round. He took it very lightly. 'But I somehow feel that Rashmi didn't like the way I was handling GD,' I said to Rohit. I didn't want any confusion between Rohit and me, so I was trying to clear it up, but Rohit asked me to stop the discussion. We returned near to the auditorium, where all other students were waiting for the result. After a few minutes, ABS HR came with a list. Rohit and I were selected, but Rashmi's name was not there. I didn't know, but somehow I felt guilty that because of my arguments in GD, Rashmi couldn't clear the round. Rohit hugged her to give her support. I was feeling hesitant to talk to her. Rohit asked her to go to the hostel to take a rest. As soon as Rashmi left, I tried to talk to Rohit, but he was not interested to talk to me regarding the same issue. This behaviour of Rohit was killing me from inside. We all were ready for the technical round. It was Rohit's turn; he had finished that round in twenty minutes and got selected for the next one-on-one technical round with the manager. He called Rashmi and gave her news of his selection. In between, my turn came. I went inside with a lot of tensions because of Rashmi's rejection and Rohit's behaviour by avoiding talking to me about the GD round issue. I didn't know what happened to me that time. I was completely blank and couldn't perform and was rejected.

When I came outside, I couldn't find Rohit. I asked other batch mates; they informed me that Rohit went for the fourth round. I decided to go to the hostel rather than wait there. I left the placement department and came directly to the hostel. I tried to sleep, but I couldn't get asleep even after one hour's try. Because of my mind tsunami, I was feeling restless. I smoked nearly four cigarettes but couldn't get relief, so I decided to go to the placement department to find out Rohit's situation. As soon as I entered, I saw a bunch of students were celebrating. As I went near, I saw Rashmi with Rohit. Rohit was very happy, and then I got to know that Rohit was selected. I felt so good, but then why didn't he come to the hostel to inform me? Rashmi was there with Rohit, and both were so happy. First time I felt separated from my own group. Rohit didn't care to inform me. He must have called Rashmi so he could give her the message to inform me. I was so confused. I decided to leave from there, but before I could do so, Rohit saw me. I went to him and congratulated him for his selection. I was feeling the odd man out in that group. First time I was feeling so weird, even after knowing that Rohit was selected for the ABS corps.

Worries No End

Day by day my frustration was increasing as my other friends were getting offers from various companies and still I was struggling. It was a lazy Sunday. I got up late and found myself alone in the room. Rohit got two offers, and from the first company he got internship also, so he didn't have anything to study. He was a free bird. Slowly I felt a gap between Rohit and me. His world was Rashmi only. He never bothered to guide me, and I also stopped taking his advice. I was feeling so frustrated. What if I could not clear any campus company? What if I would not get any internship offer? To avoid all the questions, I lit up my cigarette.

I waited till 1.30 p.m. for Rohit for lunch, but then I alone went down to the mess for my lunch. After lunch, I went to the library to study for Monday's interview. I somehow liked the library because of much peace. Suddenly Rohit came with Rashmi to the library; they asked me to come out. I came out and was about to give the room key, but before that he started shouting at me, saying I could have waited for him at room only. Why had I locked the room and come to the library? I was shocked after his argument and I didn't want to argue, so I said sorry and gave the key. Rashmi was silent and didn't stop Rohit. I went back to my seat and started focusing for Monday's interview. I wanted my friend to be with me and guide me for clearing the interview, but he was least bothered. I started reading for the next day. Till evening, I prepared for the next day and left the library. Before going to the room, I came to a garden corner for smoking. I saw Rohit and Rashmi, Rohit was teaching some aptitude problem to Rashmi. I decided not to disturb them, but I felt so bad. He could teach her in the library so that I could also learn from Rohit. From the first company's GD round, Rashmi's behaviour had changed towards me. Maybe this was the reason Rohit also changed.

Monday morning, I got up and found that Rohit was not in the room. Maybe he went for breakfast, but this early? No way. I tried to divert the focus from Rohit and decided to freshen up and be ready for the interview rounds. After breakfast in the mess, I reached the placement department. I found Rohit there with Rashmi. He was giving her guidance regarding the various rounds. For the first time I decided to tell him why he was doing this to me, but then somehow I stopped myself. After seeing me, he came to me and wished me good luck, which anyway I required. I gave a smile and went inside the auditorium to attend the company's presentation. I sat with Shruti; Rashmi was sitting in first row. After the presentation, we all moved to the exam hall for the first round, but the company HR came to Rashmi and took her out. Everybody was shocked by this, but I decided to focus on my first round. I came out after finishing my first written round; Shruti joined me. I was not able to find either Rohit or Rashmi. After one hour, the result was announced. I heard my name, but I was shocked to listen to Rashmi's name. I was not able to find out how come her name came in the list when the company HR took her out before finishing the first round. Next round was the group discussion round.

I was praying that Rashmi should not come into my team. I was lucky this time; Rashmi and I were in different teams. After the GD round, I went outside to smoke. I found Rohit smoking there. With the surprise, I asked how come he was smoking. Was there any tension? I asked about Rashmi. He told me that she was giving her manager technical round. I was in shock how come she was in the fourth round without finishing the first three rounds, but then I decided not to ask Rohit. 'Best of luck, Rahul do well!' Rohit said to me. I returned to the placement department for the result. I was selected. I was just three rounds away from the job. First time I was praying that I should be selected. When I was about to go for the third round, Rashmi came out with a big smile on her face. She ignored me, Shruti, and her other friends; we all were waiting for our third-round turn. She directly went to Rohit. Both were so happy. Rohit came to me and Shruti to inform us that Rashmi cleared all the rounds and was selected for the company. I wished Rohit and then walked towards Rashmi and wished her congratulations. We all were shocked. They both left. I was missing my friend Rohit.

Shruti's turn was first for the first technical round, and after that my turn was due. After twenty minutes' discussion, Shruti came out with big relief on her face. She informed me that she was selected for the fourth manager technical round. I went inside with mixed emotion. After twenty minutes, a technical member asked me to wait outside. Generally, if your technical round went well or bad, the technical panel would tell results immediately. I was surprised by his answer. I didn't have any choice but to wait. After all the students finished their rounds and after three hours of waiting, I decided to enquire about my result. I went inside and met the same guy who took my technical round, and he told me that I was not selected. I was so disappointed. I was about to leave the place, but then Shruti came and hugged me with excitement. She was selected for the company. She asked my result, but before I gave any answer, she read my face and told me not to worry. 'Don't worry, Rahul. We will share my salary.' She tried everything to reduce my worries. I hid my pain and tried to gel with her in her success. She asked me that today we all four would celebrate. To be very frank, I didn't have any mood for any celebration, but sometimes we have to hide our true feelings and have to live multiple lives.

I returned to the room with a disappointed heart. The room was locked. I didn't have the key. I waited for Rohit for half an hour, but he didn't come. I then went to the placement department to search for him but couldn't get him. I then searched in the garden and all locations where he could be but couldn't get him anywhere. I decided to call him from PCO. He cut the phone. I again called him; this time he picked up. I asked where he was, as I needed the key; he told he was coming in half an hour and hung up. He did not even ask about my result. I went into the garden, and suddenly I noticed wetness near my nose. I was crying, I was unable to stop the tears.

Expect the Unexpected

Day by day I was losing my confidence level. I decided to go back to Jaipur after sixth semester's project or search some small company there only, for a sixth-semester project. Almost everybody in the class got placed.

Now I started attending the off-campus as well, but the off-campus had thousands of students, and moreover, off-campus had in the last two years passed out students also. I almost lost the hope of getting a job. It was Sunday, and I woke up early, but then I again tried to sleep but couldn't get the sleep, so decided to listen to music on the system. Rohit was sleeping; after some time, Rohit's mobile rang. It was on vibrate mode. He was in deep sleep, so I just checked his mobile. It was a call from Rashmi. I ignored it and went back to the system. Again after five minutes Rashmi called, but Rohit was in deep sleep. This time also I ignored it, but immediately after the second call she called again. This time I picked up the phone. 'Rohit, please come to girls' hostel,' Rashmi said before I could speak. I told Rashmi that it was me, not Rohit. She asked me to wake up Rohit; she wanted to talk to him. I shook Rohit so that he could come out of the sleep. He was in half sleep. I told him that Rashmi was on the line and she was sounding tense. Immediately Rohit took the phone. After their conversation, Rohit got up and washed his face and started walking out. I asked what happened. He told me Rashmi's father was not well and she had to leave for her hometown. He was going to drop her off at the airport. I asked whether he wanted me to come along with him, but he told he would handle it. After Rohit left, I returned to bed for some more sleep.

Rohit returned after three hours. I asked him what happened suddenly. He told me that Rashmi's mother called her in the morning, saying her father health was not good and was hospitalized so she wanted Rashmi to be with them. Rohit was looking so tense. 'He will be fine, don't worry. She will be back in some days.' After a long time, we both were going for lunch in the mess together. Tuesday we had one more good company for campus selection. I wanted to clear this time without fail. So after lunch I decided to study in the library till evening and prepared everything. Rohit was dull and went to sleep, and then I left for the library.

Rashmi reached her home; to her utter surprise, his father welcomed her. She was totally shocked. Not able to understand why her mother called her saying her father was not well. When she entered her home, she was more shocked to see lots of her relatives already waiting for her. She was totally confused and a bit angry also at her parents. They could have called her directly rather than giving her false news. Before she could understand anything, her aunt asked her to freshen up quickly and wear a sari. She was in full anger for this drama, but still she was not able to understand the reason why all her relatives were gathered at her home and why her aunt asked her to wear a sari. She wanted to call Rohit, but as her father didn't know that Rashmi patched up with Rohit, she couldn't call Rohit. She was in tension as Rohit asked her to call him immediately once she reached home. She decided to switch off the phone as her father didn't know that still she had Rohit's mobile, but before that she sent him a message that 'I have reached home and will call you soon, please don't call'. She then asked one of her cousins for what occasion all were gathered here. She told her that 'one of the family is coming to see you for marriage'. She was in deep shock after listening to this. She immediately called her mother to check what all was going on there. Her mother told her not to worry; it was just formalities, as the boy's family was very well settled and nice. 'We are not doing your marriage, you just meet the boy and then we will decide after your graduation over.' She wanted to refuse, but before she could speak anything, her mom left to attend to other guests. She was forced to face this situation.

She wanted Rohit to be there to handle the situation; she started crying alone, but nobody was there to listen to her pain. She got ready in a pink sari. She was looking like an angel, Soft face with rounded cheek bones, proportionally slim nose, high-trimmed brows, soft pouty pink lips, and rounded chin were complemented by her easy, charming smile. Anybody who looked at her could fall into her beauty. Soon the boy's family had reached. She was in her room and asked to remain there until guided. Rashmi wanted to run away from there. Her mother came to her after half an hour and took her to the kitchen. She asked to come up with tea and snacks. She was feeling very awkward in her own house. She was shocked to see the boy. He was the same guy who took Rashmi's final technical round; now Rashmi understood the game. It was told to her that because of her second rank, she was directly shortlisted for the technical round. After some time, Rashmi's parents asked them to talk separately. Rashmi took him to her room. Guy introduced himself as Aaman and told her that it was her father's plan.

'Rashmi, you are so intelligent, doesn't think that because of all this I have selected you for my company. Actually, your and my father were old friends, when your profile came to me for marriage, I was about to come to your college. So I decided to meet you there, but after seeing you, I never had the courage to say anything,' he explained to Rashmi. 'I can understand your state of mind, but I am also feeling nervous. Please talk to me.'

Rashmi thought to tell everything to him about Rohit. But before she could talk anything, Aaman's sister entered. 'Hi, Rashmi, myself Kajal. Aaman's younger sister, hope I haven't disturbed you people. Bhiya to aap ko pehele bar dekhte he bold ho gave the! I like you as my Bhabhi.' She left after saying this to Rashmi. Rashmi was shocked and not able in her state to react to anything.

They both came out, and then Rashmi father's asked Aaman about Rashmi. He just blushed. This meant he liked her. Everybody started wishing each other for finalizing the knot. Nobody bothered to ask Rashmi. Both families had decided the engagement would be done in next one or two days and marriage after Rashmi's graduation. After all the guest left, Rashmi decided to talk to her parents. Rashmi went to her parents' room; her father hugged her and started crying in joy. Before she could say anything, her father started a conversation. 'Beta, I am sorry to call you like this. I know Aaman family very well. Aaman father and I studied together. They are such a nice people, and you will be very happy. Moreover, you will be joining Aaman's company only. You both will have a great future. Thank you, beta.' Rashmi kept silent. She couldn't able to say anything and broke into tears, which her parents took as acceptance.

She was in confusion what to do; after thinking till 2 a.m. She took her phone and switched it on. She was shocked to see twenty-two messages from Rohit. She read all the messages and called him. Rohit picked up the phone immediately. He didn't sleep; he was waiting for her call. She started crying without telling him anything. Rohit got scared; he asked many times what happened. 'Anything serious? How's Uncle's health?' But she was continuously crying. After some time, when she was a bit OK, she told him her father was healthy, that nothing happened to him. She told everything to him, what had happened in the evening. Rohit was in shock and didn't understand what to say. Rashmi informed him that within two days, they were planning for engagement.

'You please do something, I want you in my life, nobody else,' Rashmi said to Rohit and hung up the phone.

Rohit didn't understand what action he could take now. He woke me up and told everything to me and asked for my suggestion. I was not able to think anything except to inform his parents. But even if Rohit informed Uncle and Aunty, was it possible to take any action in a day or two? I was not able to think of any other solution. Rohit called Rashmi, but her mobile was coming switched off, which made him more anxious. He decided to go to her home by flight. I was not in favour of Rohit's decision. But he had to do something in one day only. I told him to tell his parents at least in the morning. It was four in the night, and after this news we would not get any sleep. Rohit switched on the computer to check the morning flight to Bhopal. The 8.30 flight was there. Rohit booked the ticket. He called Rashmi to inform her about his trip. Rashmi picked up the phone but was not sure what Rohit could do going there, but Rohit told her that he wanted to meet Uncle once. Rashmi also didn't have any way out left. Rohit took the full address from Rashmi and asked her not to worry; he would be with her in a couple of hours.

Early morning, I dropped Rohit off at the airport. I told him so many times that at least he should inform Uncle and Aunty about his trip, but he told he would manage. I asked him to call me as soon as he reached her place and call me for any emergency. I was a bit worried about Rohit. Rohit took very bold steps by visiting Rashmi's parents in this condition. He was a true partner for Rashmi, at least. When she required him the most, he proved himself by taking such bold steps. I think love gives you immense power to take such a bold decision. Tuesday was the big day for me; this company would be one of the last few good companies left on campus. But because of the Rohit tension, I was sure that I couldn't much focus on this company. I returned to the room after dropping Rohit off. I planned to study in the room only, as Rohit would call me at the hostel's office only. He would reach Bhopal by 9.45.

I was not able to focus on tomorrow's company. It was 10.30 but Rohit didn't call me yet. I was very tense. I came out for a smoke and then went to call Rohit. After the smoke, when I called him, his number was coming switched off. What the fuck? What could have happened there? At least he could have called me to inform me that he had reached her home. I felt an urge to kick Rohit's ass if he were in front of me at this time. But then I thought that he must be busy with Rashmi's family.

I was unable to study. Till 12 I didn't get any call. Physically I was in Ahmedabad, but my mind was thinking what could have been going on there at Rashmi's house.

At 3.00 p.m., when I was listening to music as I was not able to study, the hostel cleaning boy came to say that I had a call. I rushed with the speed of light. It was Rohit; he asked me to come to Bhopal ASAP. I was shocked to listen to this. 'What had happened there? Why you want me to come? Is everything fine? Where are you right now?' I started showering lots of questions. Rohit told me that as soon as he reached Rashmi's place, his father called the police and handed him over to them. Rashmi's father didn't listen to anything. Rashmi tried to solve the matter but was not allowed. Her father even called my parents and they would come by night.

'If possible, please come. I need you the most.'

'If you gave a message, please drop the call,' a high voice came from the background.

When I asked where he is, he told me he was in the police station. 'What? Don't worry, I will be there ASAP.' I took the police station's address from him. He disconnected the line. My mind was spinning. I came to the room and started checking for a Bhopal ticket. Before booking the ticket, I thought to call my parents to check the situation. I came to PCO and I called my parents from there.

My sister picked up the phone. I asked her if Rohit's parents told them anything. She told me yes; they were in tension. At 8.00 p.m. they have flight. She asked me whether I was also going. Before I could tell her anything, she told me, 'Bhiya, you also go, as Rohit's parents are very angry on him and he may be in big trouble.' I hung up the phone. I then thought to call Rohit's parents but then dropped the idea. I checked the ticket; there was one 6.30 flight for Bhopal.

I booked the ticket, and then I had to inform the placement department that I couldn't attend tomorrow's campus selection. I wrote a letter to the placement department and gave it to my class friend, and one copy I put it into the placement department drop box. What a fate. I had to drop out of tomorrow's company selection. I was feeling very bad about dropping from the campus selection. But I had to be with Rohit. I boarded the flight and reached Bhopal by 8 p.m. I directly went to the police station. Rohit was sitting inside the small lockup. He was looking very depressed and shattered. I enquired from the police inspector what could be done so he would be out of this mess. The police told me that 'there was no FIR registered, but due to Rashmi's father's contact, we took Rohit from there'. I requested for the police to please get him out of the lockup at least, because his parents would come in another couple of hours, and if they would see this, they would be in deep shock. After my request, the police took him out and asked us to wait in the sitting area. As soon we came to the sitting area, he started crying like a small baby. Even I was not able to hold myself. The police told me that once Rohit's parents had come, we needed to write one apology letter, and then they would release Rohit.

Dreams Come True

Eleventh of November 2005. The date decided for Rashmi and Rohit's marriage. Rohit got his internship in ABC Corps. Rashmi also got her internship. I applied through off-campus and finally got my project for the sixth semester with six months of probation, and if they liked my performance, they would hire me.

Only five people couldn't get a job from campus; I was one of them. But finally, I got into a small company for my sixth-semester project work. It was time to join our respective companies. Rashmi and Rohit got into the same city, Bangalore! I had to join a Pune-based company. Shruti got into FLS Soft, Hyderabad.

The journey to Rohit and Rashmi's marriage date was amazing. When Uncle and Aunty reached Bhopal, we all decided to visit Rashmi's place in the morning and try to talk with them. Initially Rohit's father was very upset with Rohit's behaviour and this unplanned trip, but after seeing Rohit's condition, he agreed to talk to Rashmi's family once. We had booked two rooms in Bhopal's hotel near Rashmi's place. When we reached Rashmi's place, already Aaman's family was present there to fix up the engagement date. After seeing Rohit with us, Rashmi's father got angry, but he didn't want Aaman's family to know what had happened last night. So he welcomed us and introduced us as his friends to Aaman's family. Rohit's father also kept silent, and they arranged breakfast for us. Rashmi's father didn't want Aaman's family to know about Rashmi and Rohit. We were not able to see Rashmi. Rohit called on her mobile, and she picked up the phone. 'Where are you, Rohit? Please take me from here.' Rohit told her that he with his family and me were sitting in her living room. After hearing this, Rashmi immediately rushed to the living room and hugged Rohit in front of all. It was like watching some Hindi movie scene. 'What's going here?' Aaman shouted in anger. Aaman's parents stood up in shock and anger. Rashmi's father came close to Rashmi and slapped her for her act. Aaman's family understood the situation. Aaman's family said to Rashmi's father, 'We should think on this matter after some time,' and left the home. Rashmi's father was about to call the police, but then Uncle stopped him and asked him to sit and talk in a peaceful manner.

Rashmi's father was in full anger and refused to talk, but then Rashmi's mother intervened and took her husband inside for some talk. Rashmi was dragged into the room by her father. I was so scared, and even Uncle and Aunty were in tension. Rohit took such bold steps. After half an hour, Rashmi's parents came to the living room with Rashmi. They looked very shocked but silent. Rohit's father started a conversation by saying even they didn't know about Rohit and Rashmi. 'Please forgive my son for his sudden visit like this, but please try to understand from our children's perspective. Even for us, it was a shock when last night he called us and told all the story. Now the time has changed, and our children never involve us in any big decision.' Rohit's father told them this in a sarcastic way. 'But as parents our duty is to guide them. We just came here to say that we are ready to think for this relation, and it is up to you, because Rashmi is your daughter and you have full right to take any decision. Please forgive my son.' Rohit's father stood and was about to leave after his conversation with Rashmi's parents. I didn't know how to react, but why was Uncle leaving the place before any decision? We all went to the main gate of Rashmi's house, but then suddenly Rashmi's father asked us to wait and have more discussions over lunch.

I took a relieved breath. Rohit and I came out from there. I hugged Rohit and told him, 'Now you don't worry, aaj to rista pakka kar ke jayege.'

He hugged me and started crying and said, 'I am sorry, bro! When you require me the most, I left you to enjoy my life. Please forgive me. Even today you drop the company's interview and stood for me. Thank you so much, Bhai.'

Even I started crying after that. We checked that nobody was watching us, and then we lit the cigarette which I kept secretly. Rohit called Rashmi from there; she picked up the phone, but her voice was still low. 'Rashmi, don't worry. I will go only after our marriage date will be finalized. I love you very much!' After our smoke, we returned to her house. Rashmi was sitting with her parents.

Rashmi's father was looking a bit soft now. He started a conversation with Rohit's parents. 'I have only one daughter, and we were planning to search for the good boy in our community. We already have searched Aaman, and they were our family friend, but because of Rohit and Rashmi, that nice proposal has to end up here. Now I have to face my community also. Moreover, Aaman was one who selected Rashmi in her campus. I don't know what they would take action.'

Before Rashmi's father spoke anything, Rohit's father started, 'Rohit is our only son, and whatever we have, it's for him only. I am a businessman and never impose any of my decision on Rohit. He wants to study, so I allowed him, and by God's grace he got into the good company. Even I want to retire from my business. I can guarantee you that we would treat Rashmi as our own daughter.'

Rashmi's mother told them that they are 'Brahmin, but your family is Vaishnav. We need to think.'

Before anything could go wrong, Rohit stood up and held Rashmi's hand and in front of everybody promised that he would take care of her very well. He would never leave her alone in any of their problems. After one hour's discussion, finally both families were ready for their marriage. I took a relieved breath. It was decided that next day they would hold the engagement, and then a marriage date would be decided soon.

Rashmi's father arranged our stay in one of the best hotels near their house. Rohit was very happy; after such a big struggle, finally they both would be together forever. Next morning, we reached Rashmi's house at the given time. Her father organized a small get-together at the nearby community hall. Rashmi wore a nice blue-coloured lengha. She looked like a *pari* from heaven. She was having very light make-up. That day, her glow was giving light to the sun. Everybody was praising her. I was feeling very satisfied for both of them. One thing I realized that day, if you want to achieve something, you have to work hard and never give up. That time, when Rohit was planning to come to Bhopal, his steps were looking idiotic to me, but when I was seeing in the back, he had done justice to his decision. We had to believe in our dots in life, and we should always connect them, having faith that in the end all the dots would be connected and create a beautiful picture.

After the engagement, we three took good pictures. Rashmi asked me that she wanted to talk to me. She said sorry to me, even Rohit told me, but I had only three words to say. Congratulations, Bhiya and Bhabhi.

Happy Time

It's time for me to leave Ahmedabad and relocate to Hyderabad. The students who got the project in Ahmedabad could stay in the hostel, but most of us got a project out of Gujarat. Shruti got the project in Bangalore only. She got into her uncle's company only. She was out of that five students who didn't get into the campus. At least that was the common thing between Shruti and me. We all four decided that first we'd go to Bangalore to search for a good temporary accommodation for Rohit, Rashmi, and Shruti, and then I'd leave for Hyderabad.

We all four booked the flight to Bangalore. Rashmi and Rohit were an official couple. They were so happy with each other. We reached 11 a.m. in Bangalore. January 10, 2005, was the joining date for Rashmi and Rohit. Shruti could join anytime, as it was her uncle's company. For me, I opted for the January 12 date. We reached 5 January in Bangalore; we had 5 days to search for a good place. We came with our seniors' references, so I thought searching for a good place wouldn't take much time. Bangalore weather was awesome. If heaven ever existed, I think it would be in Bangalore. Cool breeze with lots of greenery. I felt envious about the three of them. Bangalore is famous for its pubs. It's called Pub City also.

First day, only we got one-month accommodation in PG, which our senior suggested. Three independent rooms in the same building. We purchased all the necessary stuff from the nearby supermarket. We decided to party in the pubs. We met PG neighbours; all were working in the various IT companies. Somebody suggested the Blue Moon Pub at Bridge Road, is famous for its music. It was a karaoke club. We have reached 9.30 at the Blue Moon Pub. It was pretty dark inside. We got a corner table. First time in my life we had come to a pub. From a distance I saw one pretty hot girl was singing 'We Belong Together' of Mariah Carey. We had ordered chilled Breezer for girls and beer for ourselves. We all were enjoying. There was a small area where only couples could go and dance. I checked that the crowd was pretty decent; most of them were from IT. I made up my mind to shift to Bangalore ASAP. After finishing one round of drinks, we all four decided to dance. Initially, I a bit hesitated to dance with Shruti, but when she pulled me from my chair, I agreed. First time I was seeing the new avatar of Shruti. She was looking gorgeous in the dim light. Her fragrance was making me higher. First time I was so near to her. Rashmi and Rohit were lost in each other and dancing like nobody was watching them. There were other couple who were dancing like mad. One thing I realized about Bangalore, its people were so nice and nobody was bothered about what others were doing. Rohit kissed Rashmi while dancing, which I and Shruti both noticed. Shruti was blushing and telling me not to see there, let them enjoy. I never realized when I came so close to Shruti; she closed her eyes and said, 'I love you, Rahul.' We kissed each other. It was my first kiss, and I never realized when it turn into a passionate smooch. After the dance, we returned to our seats. I was in shock and guilty for what I had done, but Shruti was in a good mood. I didn't want to be a spoilsport, so I kept quiet. Rohit told me to sing a song for us, but I was not able to come out of shock. Shruti insisted for me to sing something and kissed my cheek, which gave a shock to Rohit and Rashmi. I went near to the desk and asked the DJ to play *Diwana* songs of Sonu Nigam. He started the karaoke version and I started singing. From afar I was able to see Shruti's reaction; she was enjoying my song and thought I was singing just for her. Then Rohit sang a couple of songs for Rashmi. We left at 12.30 from the pub and booked an auto for our PG. We never enjoyed that much. On the way, Rohit and Rashmi were making fun of Shruti and me. The girls slept in their respective room as soon as we reached the PG. Rohit and I came to a terrace for the smoke. Rohit told me that Rashmi and he saw when Shruti and I were kissing. He asked me why I never told him that I loved her. I narrated the entire story how it happened. But from that day, I had changed the way I was seeing Shruti. I liked her in the past for her energy, full-of-life attitude, but I never had any feelings for her. But after that day's incident, I also felt something for her.

Morning. We decided to visit their campus to check the route and all. Morning, first thing I had done was to tell all the truth to Shruti. 'Shruti, I always liked you, but I never had any feelings for you, but after last night, I was forced to change my way of thinking. I don't know what is love, but if being with with you is love, then I love you, Shruti.' We hugged each other. We all enjoyed the five days with one another, and then I came to the airport for my Hyderabad flight. All were upset, and Shruti was crying. I also didn't want to leave them, but I promised all that I would be in Bangalore after the internship.

Time flew very fast; already two months were over for the internship. Rohit and Rashmi finalized one two BHK house for them to stay together on April 2005. They didn't inform their parents about the house, as officially they could stay together only after marriage. They planned to shift into the new house from first of May. During these fifteen days, Rashmi and Rohit purchased all the necessary items for the house. After office hours, Rashmi and Rohit used to visit the house daily for one or other work. They themselves painted the house with multiple colours. The living room was painted in a bright goldern yellow colour. Their bedroom they painted in a sober light-blue colour. The guest bedroom was painted in a bold and bright red colour. Weekends generally went to shopping for various items to decorate their home. During these fifteen days, Rashmi purchased very small items which made the house more elegant. They purchased cute hangings, a couch with a modern look with an odd number of pillows. No more furniture except the couch and one small dining table. They gave a very breathy look for their house. They both decorated the house so beautifully. They decided to throw one good party for their colleagues at their new house. They had invited me, but I couldn't come because of leave problem. First of May, the day when they both started a new life in a new home. Shruti decided to stay in PG only till I had come to Bangalore after the internship. I called Shruti on the same evening, and she told me that she had attended the lunch party by Rohit and Rashmi and they both were looking very happy. 'Rohit was missing you very much during the party,' Shruti informed me. I promised her to join the gang very soon after the internship.

It was their first night in the new home. Rohit planned a big surprise for Rashmi. He secretly purchased Rashmi's favourite rose wine. He saved some money from his internship and purchased a gold ring for Rashmi. After the dinner, they both were sitting in the balcony with dim light and lots of glittering stars. Rohit asked Rashmi to sit there only. He went inside to arrange the surprise. He first went inside the bedroom and lit all the scented candles which they had bought. Then he went inside the kitchen to get the wine. He then called Rashmi to the bedroom. Rashmi was amazed to see the new look of the bedroom. Rohit poured rose petals on the bed, the dim light of the candles with its seductive aroma making the room full of love. He then gave the glass of wine to Rashmi. Before they could toast, Rohit bend to the knee and once again proposed to Rashmi with the gold ring. Rashmi was in tears of joy. She hugged Rohit. They finished a full bottle of wine. Wine, rose petals' fragrance, and dim light of the candles showing their effects.

Rohit pushed Rashmi to the wall. She was leaning towards the wall, Rashmi brushing her lips with his. Gently Rohit explored her face with his fingers as a blind man might as if he had never seen it before and might never again. Rashmi wanted to touch and kiss and hold him from the day she'd met him. She wanted Rohit to burn for her.

Rashmi grasped the edges of his shirtfront and, in excitement, tore his shirt from the front. Rohit removed her T-shirt and bra and pulled her against him, pressing her bare breasts to the powerful chest she'd exposed. His heartbeat was in rhythm with Rashmi's heartbeat. Rohit held her head and started devouring her kisses. Rohit stripped away her bottom in the same frantic moment. Their hands became tangled, tearing at his trouser buttons. Wool ripped and buttons tore from the cloth. He pushed her legs apart with his knee. She felt the hard shaft throbbing against her thing. They both were lost in the ocean of love. Rohit was deep inside her and was about to experience the pleasure of love; he increased his speed. Rashmi was notching his back. Soon pain aloft and both were about to reach the height of love. The first time they both enjoyed such a lovely pleasure together. Rashmi hugged Rohit very tight. Rohit gently kissed her forehead. They both were very happy with each other. A few more months to go for their marriage.

Everything Has Expiry Date

July 1, 2005, was the last day of our internship. July 15 was the final presentation day for the project. Rohit and Rashmi had the job so soon; after internship they would continue in Bangalore only. My company didn't offer me after internship, so I had to search for a job, so I had decided that after the final project presentation I would shift to Bangalore and then search for a job. We all booked our tickets to Ahmedabad for our final project presentation.

Rohit and Rashmi's family decided on 7 August 2005 for the marriage date. Rohit and Rashmi's joining date was the seventeenth of August, but they had informed their respective companies to postpone their joining by the first of September because of their marriage. They had printed cards also and posted to Rohit and Rashmi to distribute to their colleagues and college friends. Onmorning of fifteenth we all reached Ahmedabad Station. Our last official day in Ahmedabad. Ahmedabad had given us our name and our life partners. So many memories attached to this city. That Kankaria Lake, movies with friends, alcohol parties in the dry state, college bunk, ranging time, Rohit and Rashmi's struggle. Lots and lots of good memories to cherish. The first time we all were sad.

Last day in college, by twelve we had completed our presentation. Rashmi and Rohit distributed cards to faculty members and friends. Everybody was happy for them. Shruti and Rashmi had a return flight to Bangalore and Bhopal respectively. Shruti would come two days before for marriage. Rohit and I had the night train to Jaipur. I decided to take a break till Rohit's marriage and then go to Bangalore for searching for a job. Half a month was left for their marriage. All our Jaipur friends were very busy organizing various events for Rohit's marriage. Rohit's parents were very happy. Now Rohit and Rashmi were counting the days. Rohit's parents booked the train tickets for all of us for Rohit's barat. We had a superb bachelor party. We all friends enjoyed like it was our last day. Finally, the day had arrived to start the journey from Jaipur to Bhopal. Rohit's last journey as a bachelor. We had reached Bhopal three days before the marriage. Rashmi's family came to the railway station to receive us. It was a very warm welcome. Rohit's eyes were looking for Rashmi, but she couldn't come, as part of the rituals. Now they could only meet after their marriage. Rashmi's family booked one good party hall where all guest accommodations were arranged. Even Rashmi's family shifted here only for all the rituals.

Next morning, I woke up early. I wanted to receive Shruti from the airport. I asked my sister to join me. She told me, 'Where are we going?' But I decided to tell her everything on the way. I told her everything about Shruti. She was shocked to listen to this. I needed her to convince Mom and Dad. We reached the airport, but my sister stood a little far from me. As soon as Shruti came out, she ran and hugged me very tightly. I was feeling a little embarrassed, as my sister was watching us from afar. My sister joined us the very next moment. I introduced her to Shruti. Even Shruti felt embarrassed after that, but then I told her that now my sister knew about us. On the way, my sister and Shruti mingled with each other so well. We had reached the venue where all the guests were given accommodation. Rashmi already arranged for one room for Shruti. I got the key from Rashmi one day back only. I told my sister that I would be back soon. She gave a naughty smile to me and said, 'See you soon, Bhabhi.' Shruti was amazed by this word. As soon as we reached the room, I closed the door and took Shruti in my arms and gave her a tight hug. We kissed each other for the next five minutes. I told her tomorrow I wanted her to meet my parents; she was bit scared, but I told her not to worry. I went back to our room.

Next day was Rohit's birthday, so we all planned a big surprise for him for 6 August at midnight. I arranged for one beautiful heart-shaped cake. Rashmi couldn't join us because of the rituals. We all gathered at the terrace at 11 p.m. and was waiting for 12 a.m. so that we could start the celebration. It was about five minutes to 12. Before we could start the celebration, Rashmi joined us secretly and hugged Rohit. At midnight, Rohit cut the cake and fed Rashmi a big piece of cake. They kissed each other in front of all, as if we people never existed on earth. We all applied the cake cream to one another's faces. We had a great time. Rohit took Rashmi near the staircase to celebrate some private moments with each other. Even I was with Shruti behind the water tank. Shruti and I were kissing each other very passionately. We heard a sudden scream. I and Shruti ran towards the voice, and we found Rashmi in a pool of blood. We all were shocked. Rohit was screaming for an ambulance. Within a couple of minutes, both families with guests gathered. Shruti called an ambulance. Rohit was holding Rashmi's head in his lap. After some time, Rashmi lay unconscious on Rohit's lap. Soon an ambulance arrived and rushed to the hospital. I took somebody's car and went to the hospital with Shruti.

We reached the hospital in twenty minutes; doctors were informed on the way. Immediately, a senior doctor took Rashmi inside the operation theatre. Rohit broke down completely. Soon both the families also arrived. Rashmi's and Rohit's parents were deeply shocked and not able to stop their crying. Rohit told us that while going down, she slipped from the stairs. Rohit was in tears. It was very hard for me to handle Rohit and both the parents. Even I was broken. After twenty minutes of first aid, the doctor took Rashmi for a CT scan. Everybody was asking the doctor about Rashmi's condition. He informed us it was too early to say anything until the CT scan reports came. After some time, the doctor called Rashmi's parents inside his chamber. Rohit also joined them. The doctor informed them that Rashmi's condition was very critical because of internal bleeding; they needed to perform the operation immediately. They gave formality papers to sign. Rohit broke down completely; he held doctor's hands in front of the doctor and said only one line: 'Please save my Rashmi.' A team of doctors immediately started the operation. What a fate; life is so unpredictable. When we least expect anything, life hit us with hard bricks. In the morning, Rohit and Rashi were about to be tied together in a pure relation called marriage, but this fatal accident shattered all dreams.

After five hours of operation, doctors came out; everybody was keen to know Rashmi's condition. The only word we heard was *sorry*.

Rashmi had left the world. No words to describe the pain. We all were broken and in deep shock.

Dead End

Nobody was able to come out of Rashmi's incident. Rohit broke down completely and was not able to come out it. We went back to Jaipur. Rohit was not able to believe that Rashmi had passed away. He became very silent, never talked to anyone. We wanted Rohit to scream, cry so that he could come out of this grief. Rohit's world changed. He was in mourning—feeling grief and sorrow at the loss. He was numb, shocked, and fearful. He felt guilty for being the one who was still alive.

I wrote a mail on behalf of Rohit to ABC Corps to let them know about the incident and asked them if they could extend his joining date. They were ready after my follow-up. I wanted Rohit to join the company and start living a normal life. I spoke to Shruti regarding my job. She told me that in her uncle's company they would require a junior software engineer, for which she would arrange for an interview once I would be in Bangalore. After so many efforts, I convinced Rohit to join ABC Corps. We booked the ticket for Bangalore for the twenty-fifth of August, and the first of September was Rohit's joining date. Rohit's parents were in tension about him staying alone in Bangalore, but I promised them to take care of Rohit. It would be good for Rohit if he started focusing on other stuff; he would come out of this grief soon. Shruti came to the airport to receive us. We decided to stay in Rohit's house, which Rashmi and Rohit booked. Shruti dropped us off; that house was near to Shruti's PG. I was shocked to see the house; it was so beautifully decorated by them. As soon as we entered, a wind chime's sound broke my thoughts. Rohit went inside the bedroom. I went inside another bedroom to keep my luggage. When Rohit did not come out, I knocked on the door and went straight inside. Rohit was crying like a baby, hugging the pillow on which it was written 'R+R = Love'. I wanted Rohit to cry. I didn't stop him; instead of that, I went out. After half an hour, Rohit came out. He asked me to go to the pub. I felt so good; that was the first time he spoke after Rashmi's incident. I informed Shruti about our night's plan; she advised me that we both should go alone so that Rohit would feel more open and would come out of grief soon.

I decided that we would go for the same Blue Moon Pub for two reasons. One obvious reason was music, and another was, Rohit should face all the places where he had been earlier with Rashmi. We took the seat near the DJ area only; we had ordered two bottles of beer. After some time, one beautiful singer came for singing. What a voice she had. I was lost in her voice. Her voice touched our hearts directly. There was a pain in her voice. After finishing our first bottle, I asked Rohit if we should leave or not. He told he wanted to spend more time and listen to her songs. I agreed. We left at 12.30; that was the closing time.

On 29 August, Shruti arranged my technical interview in her company. I prepared well over the weekend, as I didn't want to miss the chance and, moreover, I didn't want to perform low in my girlfriend's company. After giving four rounds, I was asked to wait outside. I was scared; after half an hour one beautiful lady came out. She was in her early 30s;

she introduced herself as Bhakti, from the HR department. She took me to the conference room and asked about how my interview went. After fifteen minutes of discussion, she told me that they were interested in offering me and handed over my offer letter. I didn't know how to react. She asked me to sign one copy of offer letter and return it to her. While signing the offer letter, tears dropped on offer letter. I had waited for this moments for so long, and now it was in front of me. She left the room. I didn't have any senses left; everything came in front of my eyes, from the first day of college to the current time. I started crying. Shruti came to the conference and was shocked to see me crying. She hugged me very tightly and asked me to control myself. We didn't realize that we were inside the conference room. Finally, I got an offer. I went back home and informed Rohit about the offer. He smiled a little, which was a very positive sign. I asked him if we could party; he agreed.

This time, I invited Shruti to join us for the same Blue Moon Pub. We booked a cab, and all three of us reached the pub around 9 p.m. As soon as we entered, the same girl was singing. We took the table in front of the DJ desk. After finishing one bottle of beer, we ordered food. Suddenly Rohit stood from his seat and went to that girl and then joined her in her singing. They sang 'Chithi na Koi Sandesh'; in between Rohit broke down, and I took him back to his seat. Then we had dinner in silence. Rohit took another bottle of beer while we were returning home. We dropped off Shruti first and then came back. I didn't want Rohit to drink much, but before I could say anything, he opened the bottle and started drinking.

I was not able to see Rohit's condition, but I thought once he would join the office, he would be fine.

First of September 2005, Rohit's and my first day of the job. We both started our careers at the same day. We both woke up early in the morning and booked a cab. Shruti used to go by company cab, but it was my first day, so I booked a cab for us. Our office was on the way, so he first dropped off Shruti and me. Before getting down, I told Rohit, 'Bhai, now we are going to start our new life, so please welcome this and forget whatever happened. We can't change the past, but from today I want you to focus on your new life. I and Shruti are with you.' He gave a warm smile to us, which was a relief. I was feeling so happy that day for two reasons. First, obviously, I got a job, and second, it was in Shruti's office. We would be together always.

I returned home first. I bought sweets from the supermarket. The first day was great, finished all the formalities. My bank account was opened by the company. A bank executive handed over my debit card, on which my name was written: Rahul Jain. I was feeling so good that day. I called Rohit, and he was yet to leave the office. I thought to prepare some food for Rohit and myself. I called my mom and told her about my first day. I spoke to my sister; she was very happy. My father advised me to work with full dedication. All back home were very happy. I prepared biryani in the meantime. Rohit came after one hour. He looked tired. His day also went in formalities. We had dinner and then we went for a smoke. He was looking tired but OK. He was talking normally that day.

I dropped Shruti off at the airport after office, as she had to attend a family function. It was our first weekend. I called

Rohit for evening plans; he said to go to the Blue Moon Pub. Rohit started enjoying the pub music, I believe. We reached 9.30 at the Blue Moon Pub. The same girl was singing. After seeing Rohit, she gave *salam* from afar to Rohit. She sang 'Jab Koi Baatin Bigade Jaye'. I noticed one thing: whenever we were at the pub for whatever amount of time, Rohit was fully happy. That day, Rohit asked for her name. She told him, 'My actual name is Priya, but people used to call me Mohini here.' After the pub closed, we came down for a smoke. Priya came up to Rohit and asked for his mobile number. I noticed innocence in her eyes. Rohit gave her his number. She left in a cab. We reached home at one. I was about to go for sleep, and Rohit's phone rang. We both were shocked at who had called that late. Rohit picked up the phone, and before he could say hello, a beautiful voice on the other side told him it was Mohini. Rohit told me that it was Priya's call. I just gave a naughty smile and went back to my room.

That night, both spoke for the first time. Priya asked him why Rohit always looked so depressed and tense. That night, Rohit spoke to her almost till morning and told his entire story to her. When I woke up in the morning, Rohit was sleeping. He was looking so peaceful while sleeping, and I observed that after so many days, Rohit slept. Somebody said it correctly that when you share your sorrow, it would surely reduce.

New Beginning

December month was famous for Bangalore parties. I was planning to do a big bash. We checked a few deals for the various hotels; even Shruti was equally excited. I finalized one three-star resort for a New Year bash. When I reached home after office, Rohit had already come. He told me he was done for the day so came back early. I informed him about the New Year plan, but he told me we would go to the Blue Moon Pub. I told him at least one day we could celebrate at a good place, but he was decided that he would go to the Blue Moon Pub only.

Mornings, Priya used to study in the college and by evening she was doing this singing job at the pub, so that was the only location where Rohit could spend time with her. When I informed Shruti to drop the plan, she was bit upset. I decided that before New Year's Eve, we would go for a nearby place to Bangalore. We decided to go for Shivaganga, which was fifty kilometres from Bangalore. Shruti was not happy at all, but she didn't have a choice. I made all the arrangements for the three of us for the twenty-fourth of December, on the eve of Christmas. On the twenty-third, Friday, Rohit went to the Blue Moon Pub, but I skipped. I went with Shruti for a movie. Next morning, I confirmed the plan with Shruti and Rohit. Rohit told me that 'Priya would like to join, if you guys don't have any problem. I will also get company'. Now I was in the middle of two ways. I told him it was OK without asking Shruti. Full day, I was making plans how to tell this to Shruti but couldn't do so. Next morning, we booked a cab at six in the morning. So first Rohit and I boarded the cab and on the way we would pick up Priya. When we reached Shruti's place, she was ready with lots of packed *dabbas*. She cooked lots of things for us. She was looking so much excited. As soon as we started, Rohit guided the cab driver to go from MG Road to pick Priya up. Shruti looked stunned. I told her that Priya was also joining us. After listening to this, she pretended that she didn't have any issue, but I could read her face; she was very much upset. The cab stopped at MG Road to pick Priya up. My god, she was looking gorgeous in an Indian outfit. She was wearing a light-yellow-and-black-coloured salwar suit with a transparent dupatta. That small bindi on her forehead was like the sun giving light to the world. I had never seen her look like this; even Rohit was surprised. We had seen her in the pub with normal Western outfits, sometimes with shorts, but this avatar was the first time. She sat next to Shruti. Shruti hardly talked during the journey, which clearly indicated that she was very upset. But I couldn't do much that time. We reached Shivaganga after one hour. Rohit was very happy. We started trekking; we had to climb a mountain. For some time, we all were together, but then Rohit and Priya went ahead. I got a chance to clear the air with Shruti, on which she refused to listen to anything. I felt so frustrated when someone does not give you a chance to put your point. I finally quit. Shruti and I reached on top after one hour. We didn't find Rohit and Priya After half an hour, Shruti asked me to call Rohit and find out where they were. I called Rohit, but his phone was switched off. After waiting one hour, both came. Rohit told me that they went in the jungle to click some photos. Shruti was about to scold Rohit, but then somehow I managed the situation.

That was the worst outing I ever had. We returned home at late evening. We dropped Priya off first and then Shruti. I asked Rohit to go home. I would come after some time. Shruti and I got down at her PG. Finally, there was nobody. I said sorry to Shruti and told her that I also got to know about Rohit's plan yesterday only. She said 'hmmm', on which I got a little upset. 'Please talk to me, don't do that.' Shruti told me she would be fine after some time and I should leave this topic now. I felt so bad. She didn't bother and went to the PG. I was standing still at her PG. She went to her balcony but ignored me. I called so many times, which she didn't pick up. I came home at night. Rohit was looking very happy.

Shruti texted me sorry after two days, and I took a relieved breath. She asked me to meet after office for dinner. I informed Rohit that I would have dinner with Shruti and come late. I picked Shruti up from the office. On the way, Shruti hugged me behind the bike and said sorry. I felt so relaxed after two days. We reached our favourite restaurant. During dinner, she told me that she was fed up with PG and wanted to shift to a flat. I nodded in agreement. After dinner, on the way back to Shruti's PG, she told me she wanted me to shift with her. I didn't know how to react. She told me that near my flat there was one small apartment where we both could shift. I told her to give me a couple of days. I returned to the home; Rohit was talking to Priya over the phone. I came to my room and tried to sleep, but I couldn't get any sleep. I didn't know how to inform Rohit about this. He needed me, and Shruti also wanted me to shift with her. I couldn't be able to choose between two ways. Sometimes life would give you two choices to select and in any way, whatever you select, you would be the loser.

Anyhow, I decided to talk to Rohit about Shruti's plan. I told everything to Rohit about Shruti's plan. He asked me a simple question. 'What do you want to do?' I told him, 'I love Shruti and I'd love to shift with her, but I can't leave you alone like this.' On which Rohit told me he would be fine, and if anything, he would call me, so he advised me to shift with Shruti. I didn't know how to react. I wanted to live my life with her, but not this way. I texted her, saying that we could shift together. She was very happy on my decision. I wanted Rohit to be safe and secure. He still had not come completely out of Rashmi's incident.

New flat. I shifted with Shruti without our parents' knowledge. We both decided that after one year, we would inform each other's family. I was a bit scared, but Shruti looked more confident than me. Slowly Rohit and Priya were coming closer to each other. Priya was liking Rohit, and Rohit also started developing some feeling for Priya. One evening, Shruti had some work, so I decided to go to Rohit's flat and asked him about his feelings towards Priya. I reached Rohit's flat; he was talking to Priya, on which I told him that I needed to talk something important. He asked Priya to call back after some time. Rohit asked me what the matter was. I didn't know how to start and from where to start. I took a deep breath and asked him what was between Priya and him. He was shocked by the question and told me nothing. 'Please don't hide anything, Rohit, we didn't know anything about her. She is working in the pub as a singer, and maybe she is a good girl, but do your parents accept this truth? Does society accept her? It may be the case that you are in tension so that you attracted to her, but I don't think that you both should go further.'

He smiled at me and said only one statement. 'She is human, and she has heart, very beautiful heart, and I think I am in love with that heart. I want to tell you first, but before that only you asked me. I don't care about society and all. She is doing her job, and she told everything to me which she never shared with anyone, and once you know the fact, you will start respecting her. I need your support, Rahul, as you always stand for me.' After two hours of discussion, finally he convinced me. I told him that he should tell his feelings to Priya soon. Rohit planned to share his feelings with her by the weekend.

Saturday night, Rohit and I went to the Blue Moon Pub as planned. Priya was continuously looking at Rohit and singing each line of the songs for Rohit. Rohit gathered courage and went to the stage with gold rings which I also didn't know when he purchased. He bent down on the knee and proposed to Priya. Priya was shocked. Even I was shocked to see Rohit like this. He did it in front of almost 200 people. The pub manager came in between and asked Rohit and Priya to come into his room. I also joined them. The manager was very angry at Priya. How could she be so unprofessional? He was continuously scolding Priya. On sensing the situation, I asked the manager to come with me so that both Priya and Rohit would get enough time to talk. I explained everything to the manager outside, and finally, he agreed to my talk. But he told me, next time, Rohit should not do anything inside the pub. He could meet her outside during no-duty hours. Priya was very upset. We came to the manager's room. The manager gave warning to Priya and asked her to leave for the day. Rohit, Priya, and I came out of the pub. I told Rohit to come home directly after talking to Priya.

Priya was continuously crying. Rohit held her hand and asked her whether she loved him or not. She told him yes, but she was not from a well-settled family. People considered her a slut, and she didn't want anything too bad for Rohit because of her. Rohit simply hugged her and said he would manage everything; he just needed her support and time. Priya nodded her head and accepted Rohit's proposal. They hugged each other.

Single Ray of Hope – Current Time

I consider Shruti's suggestion and I sleep for one hour. When I wake up, Shruti orders food for all, and for me she prepares hot dal rice, one of my favourites. I am so lucky to have Shruti. I hug her. I tell Shruti that there was something wrong about Rohit and Priya's discussion. Her phone is switched off; now till Rohit tells us, we don't know what had happened between them. She also tries Priya's phone, but it is switched off. While I am having my dinner, Shruti is packing all the food in *dabbas*. I decide that once Rohit would be fine, I will ask my parents to visit Shruti's family and decide our marriage date.

After the power nap, I come back to the hospital with food. Uncle and Aunty don't want to eat. They are continuously crying. Now everything will be fine. Rohit will be fine, and they will discharge our Rohit very soon. I told so to Rohit's parent. After lots of requests, they are ready to eat something. The doctor tells us only one relative can stay at the hospital as inside ICU nobody is allowed without the doctor's permission. Uncle wants to stay, but considering their health, my father suggests that 'Rahul will stay at the hospital, and if anything, he will call us. We all should go home.' Finally, they agree. I book a cab and send them with my parents to Rohit's home at night, at 10. Once they have left, I come out for a smoke. I again call Priya, but her phone is switched off. I feel something fishy. I come back outside the ICU and call Shruti. She is also tense about Priya. What will has happened? Should we inform police that Priya was missing? Or should we enquire about her in her pub? I tell Shruti to wait for Rohit's consciousness. Shruti was tired, so she slept. I am not getting any sleep, so I start thinking what would be the reason for Rohit to go to Airport Road so late.

At 7.30 a.m., a nurse comes to wake me up. 'Rohit is in the sense, you can call his parents.' I ask if I can meet him; she tells me yes and asks me to follow the ICU rule. After getting fully dressed, which is required in ICU, I go inside. Rohit is seeing me. The tears from his eye are going down, slowly touching his cheek and then disappearing in the pillow. I tell him not to worry much; he is fine and will be discharged soon. He wants to tell me something but does not have enough strength to talk. 'Don't stress out, we will talk later. Uncle and Aunty are here, and I will inform them this good news, they will be very happy.' He asks me how he came here. Before I can tell him anything, the nurse comes and scolds me that the patient needs rest. I should not disturb him. The nurse informs a doctor about Rohit's condition and tells me that around 9.30, a doctor will come for ICU visit. That time, he will instruct us what to do next. I thank her and come out to call Uncle and Aunty. When I call them, I am able to listen to a ring nearby. I turn around and am shocked to see Uncle and Aunty so early. We all are very lucky to have such caring parents.

Both Uncle and Aunty meet Rohit. Aunty is not able to control her emotions and starts crying in front of Rohit. Rohit also starts crying. After meeting Rohit, Aunty breaks down completely. Around 9.45, a doctor came for a visit. We all are curious to know about Rohit's status. He asks all of us to come to his cabin after he examined Rohit. When we enter his cabin, the first word we hear is 'Congratulations. Rohit is out of danger. We will keep him inside ICU for next three days, and then we will shift him to normal room and do observation for next four days, and once everything will be fine, we will discharge him.' I hug the doctor. Finally, Rohit is out of danger.

'When can he join the office? I mean, when can he start living the normal life?' I ask the doctor. He tells me for next two months he should not travel, and after then, once everything's fine, he can start a normal life. Rohit's parents decide to stay in Bangalore for the next two months till Rohit will be fine. But Uncle can't stay due to business, so it is decided that Uncle will go home with my parents after three days and Aunty will stay with us. As Rohit is fine now, I told them that they can take the rest at home. I will be in hospital only. I call my team lead and inform him about the incident and take five days' leave. I also want my parents to meet Shruti. I call Shruti and ask her view on my decision. She is excited but has little fear inside. 'Don't worry, everything will be all right,' I tell her. I tell her that my and Rohit's parents are about to go home, so if she can arrange some food. She agrees after a bit of hesitation. She wants me there when she first meets my parents, but I want them to meet first without me. I had given an extra key to Rohit's home to Shruti.

At 10.30, my mom calls me that my friend has arranged breakfast for all. 'She is very sweet girl.' And she asks a few questions. How do I know her? My plan is executed successfully with Shruti's effort. I decide, before my parents will go to Jaipur, I will inform them about Shruti and my future decision to marry. Shruti calls me that my mom is very sweet, and so are Rohit parents. She tells me that Rohit's parents are very tense about Rohit and are discussing that they will take Rohit back to Jaipur once he will be fine. She is worried about Rohit's future. It is too early to say anything; maybe Rohit's parents' decision is right; he is the only son. First Rashmi's death, and then now Rohit's condition. But my worries are for Priya and Rohit's future. 'Don't worry, Shruti, everything will be fine with Rohit, tomorrow morning, I am going to tell about you to my parents,' I inform her. I learned one thing from all this incident: Do what you want to do. Tell everything that you want to share to your family, as life is very fragile. I go for a smoke and again call Priya. Same thing happens. Phone is switched off. Now I worry about Priya also. I need to find where she is. Evening, when Aunty comes, I decide to go to the Blue Moon Pub to find out about Priya.

At 7.00 p.m., when Aunty and Uncle have come, I first plan to go home, freshen up, and then go to the pub. When I reach home, my mom bombards with questions about Shruti. My father keeps silent. I tell my mom that we will talk about this tomorrow. I have some office work, so I will go to the office after dinner. I don't want to tell her about Priya, so I tell a lie. Around 9.30, I reach the pub; they arrange our regular table. But I have not come to drink today. I am not able to find Priya. I ask a waiter about Priya; he tells me that Priya Madam quit the job. I am stunned to hear that. Is that the reason for Rohit's accident? Why didn't Rohit tell me anything about Priya? I am surrounded by lots of questions. I leave the pub. I come to the hospital so that Uncle and Aunty can go home. Rohit is sleeping because of the medicine's effect. I inform Shruti about Priya. I am trying to connect all the shattered pieces but couldn't be able to connect them. Now Rohit is the only one who can tell us what could have happened. We have to wait for Rohit to recover.

Three days later, the doctor informs us that Rohit is giving a good response to the medicine, and then from tomorrow, they will shift him to a normal room. Till now Rohit hasn't spoken any word. Nobody from us are putting any pressure on him, but I am worried about Priya. It has been four days; we don't have any contact with Priya. My parents book the tickets; next day night they have a flight, as in the train they couldn't find a ticket. I didn't get any chance to arrange a meeting with Shruti with my parents. I have only one day left. Morning, it is not possible because I used to be in the hospital, so evening, when Rohit's parents come to the hospital, I can go home with Shruti. As per plan, when Rohit's parents come to the hospital, I leave the hospital and call Shruti to be ready. I will pick her in fifteen minutes. When I reach our home, I am stunned to look at her. She has a kind of understated beauty; perhaps it is because she is so disarmingly unaware of her prettiness. Her skin is completely flawless. I doubt she uses face masks or expensive products; that really wasn't her choice. She is all about simplicity, making things easy, helping those around her to relax and be happy with what they have. Perhaps that is why her skin glowed so; it was her inner beauty that lit her eyes and softened her features. When she smiled and laughed, you couldn't help but smile along too, even if it was just on the inside. To be in her company was to feel that you too were someone, that you had been warmed in summer rays regardless of the season.

I feel so lucky to have Shruti in my life. She is a bit in anxiety; so am I. I don't have any plan in my mind what to talk to my parents, but today is the only chance. I reach home. Shruti holds my hand in tension. When we reach home, my mom is surprised to see Shruti. Shruti immediately goes inside the kitchen with my mom, and I go to freshen up. My mom and Shruti become busy in dinner preparation. Indian parents are not your average parents. Many are basically helicopter parents on steroids. Many are typically heavily involved in all their children's life choices, from career to choice in spouse, and they even meddle in their children's hopes and aspirations

They arrange dinner on the dining table. I sit with Shruti and hold her hand down the table. While having dinner, I take a deep breath and tell my parents that I like Shruti and she also has the same feeling and we want to marry each other. My parents are shocked but don't tell anything to us. We finish dinner in silence. After dinner, Shruti helps my mother clean the kitchen stuff, but nobody is talking with each other. She takes permission to leave, but my mother doesn't utter a single word. I go outside with Shruti to drop her off at our flat. She is fully tense after my parents' behaviour. I hug her and give a promise that I will make everything OK. When I return, I try to ignore my parents' interaction, but my mom starts the conversation, saying, 'We can't accept Shruti as our daughter-in-law. We will find a good girl for you.' I nod my head to avoid further discussions.

I book a cab for my parents and Rohit's father to the airport and go to the hospital. The doctor tells me that after two days we can take Rohit back to home. Finally, he is out of danger and will be home after two days. They shift him to the normal room. I have many questions for him but don't know whether it is the right time or not, but I have to ask because it has been a week and we don't have any trace about Priya.

After he is shifted to the normal room, I ask Rohit what happened that night. Why did he go to Airport Road? Where is Priya? He starts crying. I hold his hand and ask him to share everything.

Big Decision

After the pub closed, Rohit was waiting for Priya to go outside. I was just having my smoke near my bike. I saw the lovely couple from afar, but today I felt something was missing in their meeting. Priya looked tense, and from a distance I could see that she was crying. Rohit was trying to console her. After a couple of minutes, Rohit came back and asked me to drop him off back home. Rohit told this to me, which I also know, but then why was Priya crying?

She was the only earning member in her family and was doing this singing job in a shady pub to support her sisters and her parents. She wanted to pursue her career in singing, and she wanted to keep herself away from Rohit because Rohit is from a well-settled family and she is from very poor family, and she didn't want anybody to pinpoint Rohit about his choice. So many times Rohit had explained to her that he didn't believe all this and he would surely give her respect and status in his family. Rohit tried to tell her that she should introduce him to her family, but each time, she refused, saying it was not the right time. She knew it would be very tough and she didn't want Rohit to suffer because of her. She got some singing assignment in Singapore, and that day was the last day in the pub, and she didn't inform Rohit about her plan. She just told him to forget her and focus on his future. Rohit felt very bad as he loves Priya very much. After I dropped him off at his home, he felt so bad and decided to convince her. Rohit called her, but she didn't pick up the phone, so he decided to go to the airport to meet her. He was fully drunk, and because of the tension, he hit the car, and then the rest was history. He didn't reach the airport also.

'Please find my Priya. I can't stay without her.'

Priya didn't share any details where she would be in Singapore.

'Don't worry, Rohit, we will do something. First you please take care of your health.'

Before I can ask other stuff, Aunty comes with fruits and food. It is the last day for my leave. I go home and call Shruti and inform her of everything which Rohit told me. I feel very bad about Rohit's condition. Why he is always unlucky in love life. Shruti understands my condition and tells me that she is coming home. As soon as she comes, I hug her and start crying like a small baby. She pampers me, asks me to control myself. 'You have to be strong, Rahul,' Shruti tells me. I tell her, if she is comfortable, I will shift to Rohit's house for next two months, as Aunty needed me. She hugs me and tells me that she was about to give this suggestion to me. I am so lucky to have Shruti in my life; she is so cooperative and understanding. I move to Rohit's house with my minimal luggage. Rohit is recovering fast, but he is depressed because of Priya. His parents don't know anything about Priya, so I generally never discuss anything related to Priya in front or Rohit's mother.

I shift to Rohit's home. Aunty is very happy. He is recovering very fast. Aunty is discussing with me that once Rohit recovers, they want him to come to Jaipur and want him to join his father's business. I don't want Rohit to quit like this and go to Jaipur; he will be more depressed. Actually,

Aunty doesn't know anything about Priya. Daily after office, I used to go to my home and spend some time with Shruti and then go to Rohit's house, and then we used to go for a walk at the apartment complex garden. Rohit wants to go to search Priya wherever he can, but the doctor told us that Rohit couldn't travel for the next two months. Daily he is telling me that we should find Priya. I have gone so many times to the Blue Moon Pub to enquire about Priya but return with no clue. Even I have gone to her home where she used to stay with her family, but that home has been given to a new tenant. We didn't have any clue where the hell she went and where her family is. I am very angry with Priya; at least she could have contacted Rohit once.

December 24, 2008

Rohit's final scan day. We book a cab and go to the hospital for Rohit's final scan. Shruti also joins us. Rohit's mother likes Shruti very much for her cooperation in the last two months. I told everything to Aunty about our relations, and she promised that she would talk to my parents once she would be back to Jaipur. It is a major relief for me and Shruti. We reach the hospital at 10 a.m. We directly walk into the radiology department. They have done all the scans and ask us to wait outside the doctor's cubicle. They would be sending a report to the doctor directly, and then we will have a session with the doctor. We all are hungry, so we go to the hospital cafeteria and order breakfast. After breakfast, we come back to the waiting area. After ten minutes, Doctor Mehta comes and calls us first. He is checking the report. 'Congratulations, Rohit, you are absolutely fine, and now you can start your normal life. You can join your office, the only thing is, you should not drive a bike for next two months because it would be little stressful to your brain. Rather you can use company transport or public transport. Enjoy the life and thank God to save you and give you new life.' We all thank Mr Mehta. On the way back home, the cab stops at MG Road signal, where Rohit is looking at the Blue Moon Pub and becomes sad.

Rohit wants to join the office from first of January, but his parents want him to quit everything and want to shift him with them and join the family business. Rohit and Aunty start arguing, on which I interrupt and politely ask Aunty that even I didn't want Rohit to quit the job. 'Please, Aunty, don't worry about him, I and Shruti are with him, and we both will take care of him.' Finally, she agrees to our request. Aunty wants me to book her ticket on the twenty-ninth of December as Rohit has also decided to join the office, but she is much worried about Rohit. But a mother always wants her son to be happy so agrees to his decision. Rohit wants to find Priya, and that was the only reason for him to stay back in Bangalore.

31 December 2008

Last day of the year. Last year, we all were together for the New Year celebration, Rohit was very happy. Rohit wants to go to the Blue Moon Pub. Shruti asks me that I should go with Rohit and give him moral support. She will go with her office friend. Each time, when I need support, without asking her she understood and always gave me unconditional support. I tell her that in the coming year we both will marry each other and our parents have to accept us. If not, we would do court marriage and then inform them. She laughs loudly and hugs me. 'Don't worry, my love, Rahul. I am only yours and our parents will understand us. Now don't worry about us.'

I go to Rohit's house; he is ready. We reach the Blue Moon Pub at 10 p.m. All are very happy to see Rohit back. We order our regular beer. Rohit goes inside the manager's room and starts enquiring about Priya, but the manager tells him that she got some singing assignment at Singapore; that is the only information he has. He doesn't know about her family. Rohit returns to the table; the same song hit Rohit, 'Tinka Tinka Zara Zara'. He immediately looks at the singer in hope that she was Priya, but it is some other singer. He is very upset and not in the mood to drink also. We return home before 12. I take four bottles of beer on the way. Rohit is in a vacuum. He wants to talk to Priya. He has many questions to ask. After a big scream, he starts crying. I somehow managed him. We both came to terrace with beer bottles. We started drinking, Rahul please search my Priya. Ask her to come back. I just want to see her and talk to her for sometimes. After that if she wants to go back she can but I can't live like this. Please give my Priya back. He was crying continuously and then fallen sleep.

1st Jan 2009

The first day of the new year, I am in a hangover and wake up early. It has been two-and-a-half months without Priya. I check Rohit's bedroom, but he is not there. I immediately go to the kitchen, and he has already woken up and is preparing tea. I tell him to prepare my tea also. I go to freshen up. I sit with Rohit, and he is looking very calm. While having tea, he tells me that he will go to Singapore and search for Priya. I am shocked at his decision, but as I know him, he always listens to his heart. He tells me that he will ask his manager if he can go to Singapore for a new project so that he can search for Priya.

5 January 2009

We both get ready for office. I ask Rohit to consider his decision once again, but he tells me he is sure about his decision. I tell him we all are with him. I also want that Rohit should get his Priya back. I tell him to give me a call once he is finished meeting with his manager. I go to my home. Shruti is waiting for me. She is ready for office. She is looking very beautiful in an Indian outfit. They have an ethnic day at the office on the very first day. I want to bunk office and want to spend time with Shruti, but it is the first day so have to go. I hug her and we kiss each other. Rather than kiss, I could describe it was the life which Shruti was transferringthrough her lips to me. I was lost in her love. We did not realize that we had not loved each other for last two months because I shifted to Rohit's apartment. It is hard to stop for both of us. She starts kissing me all over, which is reciprocated by me. She is wearing a beautiful black sari. I slowly remove the pallu and start kissing her neck; she becomes more excited and starts kissing at my ears. I lift her up and take her to the bedroom. I remove her sari and start kissing her soft breasts. She moans in pleasure. She is a tigress and takes control and comes on top of me. She starts kissing my chest and pulling my hairs. We missed each other's love very much. We start kissing each other madly. I change the position and come to her vertical lips and start kissing passionately. She moans and reaches her pleasure. Again she sits on me; slowly my thing goes inside her and she increases her speed while scratching at my chest. Soon we both are about to reach the ninth cloud. She increases her speed so much that I can feel her heartbeat at my thing inside her. Soon we both reach our love destination, and she sleeps on me after our very passionate love. We sleep half an hour in the same position and then get ready again for office. She is looking like an angel in a black sari. We hug each other before leaving home. I drop Shruti off at her office and come to my office. As soon as I enter, the receptionist greets me and gives me a very naughty smile. I don't know why she reacted like that. When I reach my desk, my friend also starts staring at me. When I go to the washroom, that time I realize that there is a love bite at my cheeks.

I am waiting for Rohit's call, so many times I take my phone to call him, but then I never dial, thinking that he might be busy with the manager for the meeting. Finally, near 4 p.m. Rohit calls me. He is happy and tells me that the manager approved his new project and next week he will be flying to Singapore. I am happy for Rohit. When you are in love you can do impossible things.

We all are busy for Rohit's shopping; it is the first time he will be going on site, but he is not that much excited because the reason was Priya. He has been given a three-month assignment, and in that time he needs to find Priya, and we all are not sure whether Rohit could find Priya. Rohit's parents are very happy to see Rohit back in action, but it was us who knew the facts. I and Shruti go to the airport to drop Rohit off late at night. He is fully confident that he will surely be back with Priya. He hugs me before leaving from Bangalore and tells thanks to me for all the support. He never did that, but he is fully emotional at the moment. I wish him best of luck.

12 January 2009

Rohit's first day to join office, but he reached on the ninth of January only. The company has arranged service apartment for Rohit with other colleagues. Without taking a rest, he goes to one of the big Indian music organizers to search for Priya. He has only one photo of Priyawith him in his mobile but returns with no hopes. On the tenth of January in the morning he listed down a few Indian organizers who are into musical events. He booked a cab and left early in the morning from one organizer to another, but no luck. He returned with an empty hand to the flat. Rohit has not even spoken much to his roommates, which are his project mates also. There are three people apart from Rohit staying there. When he returned to the flat on Sunday evening, he was looking very tense and tired. One of his roommates sensed the situation and asked if he needed any help. But Rohit didn't share anything with them. Because of the weekend, they were enjoying their drinks and offered Rohit to join them. He couldn't refuse them. After a few pages, Rohit opened up. He shared his story to all of his roommates. All were shocked to listen to Rohit story and why he was in Singapore. That night, all promised Rohit to help. They made a plan that each of them divides all the place which could relate to music. They decided that each of them would visit all the pubs, musical organizations, and all the institutions which had anything to do with music. Rohit felt a little relaxed that night.

Rainbow Has All the Colours

February 2009

It has been a month since Rohit had transferred to Singapore to search for Priya, but he could not get any information of her. It was their daily affair after office to visit various pubs to search for any of the Indian singers. Nobody got any clues. They had visited almost each and every thing. Now Rohit has decided to visit the countries near to Singapore. He called me to find out from the pub if she contacted them or not. I told Rohit that today night only I would visit the pub and find out. He informed me regarding his decision that on weekends he would travel to a nearby country and try to find Priya. Day by day his hopes were decreasing and frustration was increasing.

The very same night, I visited the Blue Moon Pub and enquired about Priya, but they had no clues. According to them, Priya told them that she was moving to Singapore, and that was the only information they had. I called Rohit and informed him. He told me that in the coming two months, each weekend they all would divide the countries nearby Singapore. The people with whom Rohit was staying were very helpful. I was praying for Rohit.

Malaysia

Rohit finished work early in the office as he had to leave for Malaysia. He left the office in the afternoon only and reached the airport. He boarded the flight at 5 p.m. A beautiful air hostess welcomed Rohit. He was not in the mood, but he greeted back. As soon as the flight started, Rohit started surfing videos in the device in front of his seat. Suddenly he got Priya's video, where she was singing in one of the pubs. It was the same song, 'Tinka tinka zara zara, hai Roshni se jese bhara'. He immediately called the air hostess. As soon as she came, he asked if she know the place and singer in the video. She identified the place, and it was in Malaysia's famous Indian pub. Rohit took the address from her. She asked why Rohit wanted that address; Rohit told her the full story. She gave her number and asked Rohit to call her back once he would find Priya, and if for any other help, he could call her back.

As soon as the flight landed, Rohit booked a cab and asked the cab driver about the address given by the air hostess. He told him that it was near behind the hotel booked by Rohit and that the pub was very famous. Each night they organized an Indian musical night. Rohit decided to keep the luggage at the hotel and then go to that pub. As soon as he reached the hotel, he called me that he got the address where Priya was working. I asked how come he got this, on which he told me the entire flight story. I wished him luck. His sound was so excited and happy. Without wasting time, he freshened up and then asked the hotel reception to book a cab for him to that address. The cab arrived after five minutes. On the way, he was thinking of all the old memories and what his reaction would be when he would see Priya after such a long time. How would she react? He asked the cab driver to stop somewhere in between, from where he could get some flowers. They stopped between and Rohit personally picked Priya's favourite flower and asked to create a bouquet from that. He was very much happy. The cab arrived in front of the pub. Rohit was very happy and gave a tip to the driver. As soon as he entered the pub, a waiter allocated him a front table, from where he could enjoy the night's show with food and the best liquor. He ordered a beer with some food. A beautiful singer was singing Indian songs. He was very happy and still planning what he would say to Priya once she came. After one hour of waiting, another singer came. He called the waiter and enquired about the Priya, but he couldn't identify the name. He then remembered the first meeting with Priya, and that time, she told him her name was Mohini. He asked about any singer named Mohini. After a bit of thinking, he told him that the group left the pub three months back only. To confirm that the waiter was talking about Priya, only then did he show Priya's photo from his mobile, and the waiter identified Priya. Rohit asked him where that group went, but he didn't know anything. He told him that the pub manager might have the information. Next moment, Rohit was in the manager's room. He showed Priya's photo and asked him if he had any information. He told Rohit that around two to three months back, that whole group left the pub, and generally they booked the organizer and they arranged the group. He told that him that organizer was not professional, and they cancelled all future programs with them. He asked that organizer's details, which initially he refused to give, but after so many requests, he gave the details. Rohit called the organizer and got that the number was no more in use. He again reached the end of the road. He at least got some clues but then no idea what to do now.

Monday, he reached back to Singapore. He called me and narrated to me the entire story. He got some hopes that Priya would be somewhere in Singapore or the nearby countries. He told me that in the coming four weekends he would search with his full intents, and he was showing me that he was full of confidence that he would get Priya. But I identified the pain and fear behind his voice.

Malaysia

Rohit took two days' leave so that he would get five days in line. Wednesday night, he took the same flight from which he got a clue about Priya. He met with the same air hostess. After seeing Rohit, she came to him to ask about Priya; he told her that he visited the pub which she suggested, but Priya was no more working there. According to him, Priya must be in Malaysia only. The air hostess told him that she would note down a few famous Indian pubs and would give their addresses once the flight landed. She told him that the next two days she had off and would give company to Rohit to search for Priya. When you are lost in the dark, a single ray of light is also very important. As soon as the flight landed, as decided, Rohit was waiting for her at the exit gate. She came after one hour, after finishing flight formalities. Rohit didn't know her name also. He asked for her name. Rashmi, she told him. It gave a shiver down his spine. He was shocked to listen to this name after so long. She told him that she would drop Rohit to his hotel and then would go to her guest house and then, morning, would come to pick up Rohit. On the way, Rohit was very quiet because he was lost in Rashmi's memory. He kept calm, but from inside he broke down completely. He felt that he was locked in one room which can only be opened from outside. He was screaming, crying, but nobody was listening to him. He felt so lonely. Whenever he was about to reach his destination, life had hit with a strong brick to his head.

Morning, as promised, she came on time and called Rohit from the reception. He didn't have breakfast and asked Rashmi that first they would do breakfast and then start the search for Priya. Rohit was looking more confident because of Rashmi's support. He felt that Rashmi from the top was seeing him and she only sent this Rashmi for his help. After breakfast, they hired a cab and started the search. From one pub to another pub. From one street to another street, they searched, but no luck. They continued the same process for the next five days. At the end of the fifth day, Rohit again became fully depressed as there were no clues of Priya, but Rashmi didn't lose hope and was boosting Rohit's morale. Both had to join their respective work. Rohit thanked her for her support in the last five days; in return, Rashmi gifted him the Ganesha idol and told him to have faith in God. Rohit returned to Singapore.

Rohit's assignment was about to finish; it was a just week left before he would come to India. He called me and started crying like a small baby whose toy was broken. I was feeling so helpless that I couldn't help with anything. I just had words which could give Rohit mental strength, but I knew his condition. Nothing could give him peace except Priya.

After lots of search and struggle, he finally left Singapore. All his roommates came to drop him off and promised to continue the search for Priya back in Singapore and would update Rohit if anyone got any clue about Priya. I and Shruti came to pick him up from the airport. He was looking so dull and tense. On the way to home, nobody had spoken anything to each other. He again joined the old project which he left. Daily he went to the office, but his body just reached the office and his heart was in search of Priya. On the other hand, now Rohit's parents started searching for a good proposal for marriage. They never had a clue that Rohit was very tense and alone in Bangalore. He kept ignoring their proposal with one or other reason, but they also wanted Rohit to settle down in his life.

Rohit again started drinking much. I felt a déjà vu. He was doing exactly the same thing when he lost Rashmi. He hardly shaved, took a bath, hardly met with friends. He stopped talking with all except for official talk. He lost all hope that he could ever meet Priya once again. I and Shruti always explained to him that he should not give a penalty to himself; rather he should focus on new things. But I know he was very alone, and this was the second time he broke, and it was very hard for him to come out. He became a workaholic and alcoholic. He started most of the time in office only. I decided to take him to a psychiatrist. I knew he would not listen to me, but I had to take him to the doctor. I told him that he was spoiling his and his family's life and he should come out of this. Shruti suggested to me that I should stay with him for some time and then make himconvenience for a doctor's visit.

I again shifted to Rohit apartment, I used to come home on normal time, but Rohit comes very late daily after work and that too in drinking state. I told him so many times to come home on normal time, but he never listen to me. I decided that after dropping Shruti home I will again travel to Rohit office and get him with me. I follow this as daily practice, bring Rohit back home on time. Then on the way we purchase our beer bottle and then I use to cook. After a week, it has been a habit. Rohit couldn't stop his drinking, but at least he was talking to me. He was missing Priya so much. Finally after a week he agreed to visit the doctor. I took the appointment for Saturday.

Morning, I got up early, but Rohit was still sleeping because of yesterday's late night. It was the fifth month and we had no clue where Priya was. Rohit stopped going anywhere. The only schedule was to work till late and then have so much alcohol, which helped him sleep. Finally, in the afternoon we had reached Dr Thomas. He was looking very mature and had thirty years of experience in neurology. His clinic was looking very posh. He took us to a room, a very elegant room; there was a massager chair, light music, dim lights, chill AC. He asked Rohit to share anything which he felt to share. Initially, Rohit was a bit hesitant to share the details, but Dr Thomas knew how to get information. Soon he told everything which had happened with him. Dr Thomas was writing bullet points out of Rohit's story. The session went on for near to two hours. Dr Thomas asked Rohit to visit him on alternate days till two weeks and then follow up on a needed basis. He prescribed medicine and instructs strictly to follow without stopping in between. He asked to wait Rohit outside and asked me to wait. As soon as Rohit left the room, he said that Rohit's condition was the very worst and we had to give him moral support. Make sure that he stopped drinking and had medicine on the same time which he mentioned without break. Be with him always. Was it any serious issue, I asked him. 'Nothing much, but he is so depressed that he can do anything.' Dr Thomas told me this in a very casual manner, but then I realized that for him it daily mattered.

Evening, Rohit asked me whether I would have beer or not, on which I stopped him politely, that he was not allowed to have any kind of alcohol during treatment. He finally agreed but was looking very restless. That night, he was not able to sleep without alcohol, but I didn't allow him to have anything. I made coffee for him, which at least gave him a little release. Finally, that night at 2 a.m. he slept.

Three days passed and he was giving a good response to the treatment. Because of Dr Thomas's efforts, he was coming out of his problem slowly, but still he was looking dull. Till treatment, I decided to stay with him only. Sometimes I felt that I was taking Shruti for granted. She always supported me in all the conditions. I asked Rohit that, if he was fine, then today I would have dinner with Shruti. He told me that I had done many things for him and I should not spoil my life for him and all other nonsense. I ordered food for Rohit and then picked Shruti up from home for dinner. During dinner, I held her hand and thanked her lots for her constant support to me. Two weeks got over and Rohit improved lots. He at least stopped drinking, but he was still not coming out from Priya's aftershock. Dr Thomas advised him to change the city for a minimum one year. Rohit again approached his manager for an on-site project, but for the long term. He got it: a one-year assignment in Europe, because of his good performance in past.

Rohit came out of his trouble, but that smile on his face is missing. He informed his parents about his decision that he was flying to Europe for one year, and after that only would he decide what to do next. Next few days, I and Shruti helped him with his shopping. He was ready to fly after one week. We decided to go for one last party in Bangalore. Rohit said that he wanted to visit the Blue Moon Pub one last time. I didn't want him to go there, but after five months he himself agreed to go somewhere, so I couldn't refuse. That night at 9.30 we reached the Blue Moon Pub. The waiter was surprised to see Rohit and me after such a long time. We ordered our regular beer. Rohit was lost in that music and Priya's virtual presence. He was broken. We went home after two hours, and as soon as we entered his home, he hugged me and started crying like a small baby. I let him do that. I wanted him to cry as much as he could and then move on in his life. He slept immediately without discussing anything.

Bangalore Airport

It was 2.30 a.m.; it was very cold. Shruti and I came to the airport to drop Rohit off. 'Thank you. Shruti,' he said to her. 'You have given lots of support to Rahul and to me also. Please take care of Rahul, he is so much lucky to have you in life. I love you guys.' He left for the flight and we returned to our home. Hope Rohit will get whatever he wants in his new life; maybe Europe will give him what he deserve. Rohit reached the Netherlands, where his company gave accommodation for the first two weeks and then he had to search for accommodation for himself. He joined the office on Monday. He had a few Indian people working in his team. He was assigned a new role as principal engineer. Now he had to search for good accommodation for himself in the next two weeks. One week went in settling down in the Netherlands and finishing some of the official formalities. His team member Vrushabh promised Rohit to help in search of a home. He told him that he had a 2 BHK flat and three people staying, and if everyone was OK, he would talk to his owner, and if everything went well, Rohit could shift to his flat. Rohit was a bit relaxed after Vrushabh's help. It was a long weekend coming, as they had some local holidays. Vrushabh spoke to the other two people and owner; all were ready to accept Rohit as a new roommate. But Vrushabh told him that Rohit had to come with the full gang to roam around a nearby location in the coming weekend. Rohit had to agree. Thursday evening, Rohit decided to shift, and Friday was a holiday and they booked a ticket for Amsterdam.

Thursday night, Rohit left the office early and took all the luggage from the guest house. He reached home by 7.30 p.m. Vrushabh introduced Rohit to the other two roommates. All welcomed Rohit, and with a new member's arrival, they decided to party. Vrushabh quickly got beer cans for all. Rohit was still not that much comfortable with the other two members, but he tried to gel with them. After two hours of the party, everybody slept, as morning, 9 a.m., they had a train to Amsterdam.

At 10.30 Friday morning, they reached Amsterdam. Amsterdam mornings are really fresh. They had booked an average hotel for stay for the next three days. After freshening up at the hotel, they decided to visit a nearby area. Amsterdam was famous for embarking on a free walking tour. At noon, they found one good desi Indian restaurant. They all enjoyed an Indian meal after a long time. While paying the bill, they received two free tickets for an Indian night at a famous Indian pub at the countryside. Vrushabh and the other people were very excited about Amsterdam nights. After roaming around for three hours, they got tired and returned to the hotel. They immediately slept because of tiredness. In the evening, they decided to visit that famous Indian pub. Rohit refused to go. He said for them to enjoy. He would be at the hotel only. All other three left to the pub. Rohit ordered beer for himself. He called me. We were talking while Rohit was having beers. We talked almost for one hour. Rohit decided to sleep. He switched off everything and went to sleep. As soon as he slept, he felt a bit uncomfortable. He got up and went outside. He was feeling suffocation. He was not able to sit inside the hotel. He called Vrushabh, but he didn't pick up. He started walking and decided to go to that Indian pub. He somehow recollected the name while they were having lunch. He was in search of a cab, but at night he hardly got anything. He continued walking. He reached the red-light area of Amsterdam. It was drizzling; a chill air was blowing. Glowing lights and beautiful girls behind the windows made the red-light area brighter. Everybody was enjoying, but Rohit felt more uncomfortable after watching all this. He was feeling breathless after walking so much. After searching in the various streets, he found that Indian pub. There were four black bouncers standing at the gate. For stag entry, Rohit had to pay 150 euros. He was about to drop the plan, as it was very expensive. But he was feeling very restless and didn't have the strength to walk more, so he paid that amount. They put a stamp of the pub on Rohit's hand.

It was very dark inside. He hardly saw anything except a white light focusing on the stage. He again called Vrushabh; this time, he picked up the phone. Rohit said that he was in the pub and asked them their table. Vrushabh said to come to the front table. Rohit tried to look for a path in the dim light. He was hardly able to see anything. Suddenly a song hit his ears. 'Tinka thinka zara zara, hai Roshni se jaise bhara.' Suddenly old memories locked Rohit feet from moving. He looked at the singer, and he was shocked to see her again after so long a time. It was Priya. He went closer to the stage. He was looking at her without a single blink. It was too dark in the pub. The only light was the spotlight on Priya. He stood still near the stage. Soon he felt some wetness near the corner of his eyes. He was crying. Soon after the songs, everybody was applauding Priya's performance. Suddenly all lights were switched on. Rohit was continuously looking at Priya. She was looking more beautiful, but there was pain behind the smile. Priya was greeting the crowd, and suddenly she saw Rohit. She became still for few seconds. Both exchanged many talks with their eyes. It was hard to believe for Priya to see Rohit. She was not able to control her emotions and ran towards Rohit. She jumped out of joy and hugged Rohit. Both were not able to control their emotions. Both were crying and hugging each other. There were lots of questions to be answered, but both were lost inside each other.

'I am sorry,' Priya whispered to Rohit.

'I love you, Priya. Will you marry me?' Rohit bent down on one knee and proposed to her. She cried out of joy. When you have only love between, then millions of questions will dissolve automatically. The crowd was clueless but became emotional. They hugged again. Both didn't know how to react. Both were so happy.

Printed in the United States
By Bookmasters